CRIME
IN THE
OLD
DOMINION

CRIME
IN THE
OLD
DOMINION

EDITED BY
JOSH PACHTER & K.L. MURPHY

Contents

Introduction

Crime has made headlines in Virginia since the earliest days of the Jamestown Settlement, when George Kendall, one of the founding settlers, got caught up in the politics of the times, was accused of attempted mutiny, and was executed by hanging in 1608.

The state's history is filled with tales of despicable murders, such as the killing of Alice Knight, who was allegedly poisoned by her husband, Lemuel Johnson, on their wedding day in 1918. It seems Johnson had had a girlfriend on the side for several years. He pleaded not guilty and convinced a jury of his peers to set him free, yet ended up committing suicide in 1925.

In the late 1980s, a series of eight murders occurred along the twenty-two-mile stretch of roadway in Williamsburg, known as the Colonial Parkway. For decades, the crimes went unsolved, and local news organizations ran articles on milestone anniversaries. Finally, in January of 2024, the Virginia State Police identified Alan W. Wilmer as a suspect in three of the murders. Wilmer died in 2017, so he never had his day in court, but the news brought some sense of closure to the families of the victims, who had grieved for years.

When our chapter's leadership team first debated the idea of producing an anthology, one of our biggest questions was the collection's motif—the unifying element that would tie the stories together. Would each story integrate the commonwealth's rich history? Would we ask authors to craft stories around Virginia's broad and diverse landscape, from the Blue Ridge Mountains to the Atlantic Ocean, from the concrete cityscapes of the Metro D.C. area to the eerie forests of the Great Dismal Swamp? Or would our anthology focus on some of our state's many famous—and infamous—citizens?

In the end, we chose to give the authors the freedom to choose which of these varied elements to incorporate into their tales, with the single caveat that the crimes they wrote about must take place in Virginia. Thus, our title: *Crime in the Old Dominion.*

In these pages, you'll find a dozen tales of crime that run the gamut from murder by assorted methods—some more gruesome than others—to embezzlement, kidnapping, bank robbery, and burglary, taking readers across the state from Charlottesville to Virginia Beach.

I hope that, like me, you'll be intrigued by the settings, mystified by the whodunnits, and engaged with loving—and sometimes hating—the various characters.

Hold on tight and enjoy the ride!

Leah Price
President, Sisters in Crime Central Virginia (2023-2024)
June 30, 2024

Beach Club

By K.L. Murphy

Detective Martin leans back, lacing his fingers over his belly as though he has all day, but I'm not fooled. He's losing patience with me, and I don't blame him.

"I don't know what you expect from me," I say finally. "I told you yesterday, I'm sorry Joey's dead. I am. But we split up three months ago. This has nothing to do with me."

"Split up, or you kicked him out?"

There's an archness to his tone I don't like. "Does it matter?"

"Depends. Which is it?"

"I asked him to leave." That's the nice version.

"And now he's dead."

"Yes, that's been established."

"And his girlfriend."

I say nothing to that.

"We have witnesses who say you threatened him."

He doesn't know the half of it. In truth, even the sight of Joey could set me off, but I know that's not what he's referring to. When Joey sicced a lawyer on me in hopes he could break the prenup, it was a declaration of war. What else could I do?

"I threatened to countersue him, not kill him. He wanted more money than he was entitled to, and I told him where he could go."

"Right, the lawsuit." Detective Martin shuffles through the file in front of him. "Mr. Appleton claimed he was blackmailed into signing the prenuptial agreement?" His eyebrows rise as though there's a question. Again, I say nothing, waiting for what I know is coming next. "I believe you told him you'd see him rot in hell before you gave him one more dime. Is that about right?"

It's all I can do not to smile at the memory. Oh, how I relished that scene, storming the tennis court during his serve and waving the court papers in the air for everyone to see. Martin thinks he can use that to catapult me to prime suspect, a straight line from anger to murder. I can't decide if that makes him lazy or stupid.

I hold his gaze when I answer. "I also said my lawyers would be in touch with his lawyers and, when I was done with him, he could crawl back under the rock he came from." I lift my chin. "That's a far cry from what you're implying."

It's as though I haven't spoken at all. "You were angry at him for taking things public, weren't you? For accusing you of blackmailing him into marriage?"

Whatever I was that day, I wasn't angry. Not that I didn't have every right to be, after I discovered my husband had slept with every woman from the club with a six-figure bank account—the bigger, the better. Or later, when I learned he'd bilked my ailing father out of hundreds of thousands of dollars, having him sign checks when no one else was around.

"Let me spend time with him, Dee," he said. "Man to man. Father to son kind of thing."

The days my father was still with it were special but coming less frequently by then. I couldn't be with him twenty-four hours a day, and the nurses I'd hired welcomed the break whenever Joey showed up. "He's so devoted," they said. "So caring."

Joey was good. I'll give him that. But I'm better.

"No one blackmailed Joey Appleton into anything."

Joey would have signed away his firstborn for entrance into my family, but I didn't know that then. I thought he loved me. Even now, I can't forget the way he held my hands, his eyes searching mine. "I'll sign whatever it takes to convince you and your family that the only thing I want is you. No one and nothing is more important to me."

Touched, I offered to add language that would protect *his* company and personal wealth, but he shot it down. "Your family has owned its company for generations, but I'm a self-made man," he said. "What's mine is yours, my love."

As it turned out, there was nothing magnanimous about his gesture. His assets were mostly bogus. The offshore accounts he'd casually mentioned didn't exist. His companies were shells, with no balance sheet and no income. What a fool I was.

Joey was good-looking, but not in an obvious way. Smart, but not Ivy League. "Scrappy," my father called him, early on. I was never sure if that was a compliment. But none of that is what drew people to him.

My first husband, Harrison Burr, could rig a sailboat and choose the best wines. He collected art and cars with equal relish, but he didn't know anything about warmth and even less about me. He couldn't tell you my favorite color. He didn't know that, on cold nights, I wanted to lie naked in front of a roaring fire. He didn't understand my attachment to my fifteen-year-old tabby or my devastation when I had to put her down.

"That thing was leaving tufts of hair all over the floor," he said. "A bit nasty, if you ask me. I'd think you'd be a little relieved." Surprisingly, the shock on my face must have registered, because he added, "For Hattie, I mean."

My precious feline's name was Mattie.

Joey, on the other hand—bless his dead heart—didn't collect art and cars like my first husband, but he did a deep dive into the people he pulled into his orbit. He even quizzed me sometimes. If I mentioned I loved lilies, there would be a bouquet within a few hours. He could rattle off the names of my favorite restaurants, perfumes, and designers. He collected information, soaking it up like a sponge. He made you believe you were the only person he wanted to talk to, to be with, to touch, the only person in the world that mattered.

If I hadn't come home early from a girl's trip, I might never have learned the truth. I found him stretched out in the library, a glass of wine on the table. Van Morrison played over the speakers, and he had his phone to his ear. It occurred to me that he hadn't heard me come in. Smiling, I slipped off my shoes, tiptoeing into the room. Two steps from planting a kiss on the back of his neck, the sound of his voice reached my ears.

"Darling, you know I want to be with you. I need more time, that's all."

What the hell?

"You know how Dee is when she's home. Very needy."

The husband who claimed it was his life's mission to please me was calling me needy? My stomach twisted.

"Trust me when I say all I can think about is you. Whenever we're together, it's my favorite time of day."

Bile rose in my throat, and tears sprang to my eyes. How many times had I heard those same words?

"I'll make it up to you, Katherine. I promise."

Katherine? I couldn't breathe, couldn't speak. He hung up, and still, I didn't move a muscle. My heart pounded so loudly in my chest, I thought he'd spin around any minute, but instead, he called another of my so-called friends.

"Lila, it's me. I've booked our usual room at the Cavalier for Tuesday." There was a pause. "I can't wait, either. How's Allison? Fever gone?" Another silence on Joey's end. "That's good. I'll bring a little something special for both of you."

I finally found my legs, backing out of the room before he knew I was there. I drove around for hours, numb. I can't say where I went exactly, but I ended up at the beach, watching the waves crash onto the shore.

So Joey had used his charm to worm his way into multiple bedrooms. Maybe I could have lived with that, but these women were my friends. I played tennis at Princess Anne with Lila. Katherine and I had gone to boarding school together. How many more of them were there? Did they know about each other?

By the time the sun came up, the numbness had worn off, replaced by something far colder.

Detective Martin clears his throat, tired of waiting for me to give him something relevant. I decide to throw him a bone.

"My husband was having an affair. That's why we separated."

Martin works to keep his expression neutral, but his fingers twitch. "I see. Another reason for you to be angry with him. And maybe Ms. Camden."

"Actually, I didn't know about Beth." I lie so smoothly, I almost believe myself. Poor Beth. She'd traded one cad for another, but that wasn't my problem. I've surprised Detective Martin, though.

His forehead scrunches in a very unattractive way. "Ms. Camden wasn't the woman he was having an affair with?"

"I kicked him out because I learned he was sleeping with Katherine Smithson, my oldest friend. We met when we were in boarding school as kids. Went all the way up. We were in each other's weddings…." I let my voice trail off.

"That must have hurt," he says.

I see no reason not to tell the truth. "It did." Cocking my head as though the idea has just occurred to me, I ask, "Should I have my lawyer here?"

His gaze flicks to his partner, who has yet to say a word. "Well, this isn't a formal interview," Martin says.

Now who's lying?

"But of course, it's your right, if you think you need one. If you've done something." He lets that last word sit there.

Pretending to mull it over, my mind wanders back to the first time I saw Katherine after I knew the truth.

We went for a run on the beach, something we did regularly enough that my call didn't seem odd. I waited until we'd clocked close to two miles before I dropped the bomb.

"I know about you and Joey."

Katherine didn't even break stride. She's one cool customer. "Do you hate me?"

"Yes."

That got her. She stopped short, and I swung around to face her. Her jaw clenched and unclenched as she wrestled with what to say, but I saved her the trouble.

"But I hate him more."

She stared at me for what seemed like a long time before nodding.

"After I found out," I said, "I hired a detective."

Katherine's already flushed cheeks reddened.

"I needed to know everything he was up to and everyone he was up to it with."

Her chocolate brown eyes widened.

"Lila, for one."

Katherine pressed her lips together.

"And Julia, and Beth."

Her face darkened. "All of us?"

"Yes."

"That son of a—"

"Stop." I held up a hand. "The right to be mad about who my husband is sleeping with doesn't belong to you."

Katherine closed her mouth and stared out at the water. When she looked back at me, tears shone in her eyes. "What do you want, Dee?"

"I want you to listen."

Martin raps on the table, yanking me back to the present. "Mrs. Appleton?"

I fold my hands in my lap. "I think I *will* call my lawyer, if you don't mind."

We don't have to wait long. When Julia Hammond appears, she's wearing one of her power suits—probably Gucci—and gets right to the point. "Gentlemen, why don't you bring me up to speed?"

Ten minutes later, Martin resumes his questioning, and it's apparent this inquiry is far more formal than originally implied.

"Do you or do you not own a gun, Mrs. Appleton?"

Julia and I put our heads together, whispering, before I answer.

"Yes, I do," I say, glancing at Julia. "I mean, I did. Joey took it when I kicked him out. He said he was worried I'd use it on him."

"And did you?"

"Use it on him?"

Julia stops me. "Detective, I believe my client has already stated the gun was not in her possession, which ergo, would make your question moot."

Martin asks another question instead. "Is there anyone other than you who can verify the gun was in your husband's possession?"

I glance at Julia, who shrugs. Then I remember. "It was on his list of assets for the divorce. We were starting negotiations before he decided to sue, and the gun was on his list, not mine."

True, yet if Martin looked closer, he'd find the list was for what was to be owned post-divorce.

"Okay," he says, unable to hide his disappointment. "Let's move on."

Julia stands. "Actually, Detective, I think my client has cooperated quite enough." She places a hand on my shoulder.

Martin keeps his focus on me. "Where were you Saturday night, Mrs. Appleton?"

"You don't have to answer that," Julia says.

"It's okay." I look up at lawyer, my friend. "I want to clear this up."

Clucking her tongue, she sits down again. "Fine."

Martin repeats the question.

"On Saturday night, I went to some friends' house for dinner."

"Their names?"

"Lila and Roger Crane."

"Was anyone else there?"

"Just Lila and Roger and me."

"And what time did you arrive at the Cranes' home, Mrs. Appleton?"

"Seven, and I didn't leave until midnight."

"That's a late dinner."

I shrug. "Lila and I decided to watch a movie after we ate. *Oppenheimer.* Have you seen it?" The movie will show up in their viewing history one time only, the night Joey died.

"What about Mr. Crane? Did he watch the movie?"

"No. He was tired and had a bit too much to drink, so he went to bed. It was just me and Lila. After it was over, Lila wanted to drive me home, but I wouldn't let her. It's only a couple of miles, but we'd had some wine during the movie, so I called an Uber."

"Can you verify that?"

"It'll show up in my ride history, right?" I look at Julia. "Oh, and my driver's name was Maurice. I remember that." Details matter in these situations. I'd made sure Maurice wouldn't forget the tipsy woman who wouldn't shut up.

Martin's thumb drums the table as he flips through the flimsy file. He brought me into this room with a theory, confident he'd have motive, means, and opportunity wrapped up before lunch. He thought I wanted to make Joey and Beth pay, but he didn't know about Katherine. When he asks around, at least a dozen or more women from the club will swear I've been snubbing my oldest friend for weeks. As for Beth, I've spent no more and no less time with her than before. She's new to town, an outsider, and while I make a point of being friendly, I never go out of my way. For the most part, I see her only in passing. No one will say otherwise.

The gun, Martin's sure-fire means, is also a problem. For *him*. There's not a single witness who can put the murder weapon in my possession rather than Joey's. More reasonable doubt.

The detective picks up a page, starts to say something, and changes his mind. He didn't bank on Lila and Roger, either. Or Maurice. If my alibi checks out—which it will—opportunity also goes up in a puff of smoke.

Julia and I wait in silence. Martin's frustration is etched into the lines around the corners of his mouth, giving him a hangdog look that does nothing to improve his appearance. Eventually, he closes the file. "Thank you, Mrs. Appleton. That's all for now."

Back at my house, I sink onto the couch. "Now what?" I ask Julia.

She kicks off her shoes. "They'll go to Katherine, but that will only bring them back to me, since she and I were together all night, planning a surprise party for Maryellen. Sarah and Kim will back that up." She grins.

"You have the takeout delivery receipts? The guy saw everyone?"

"Exactly as we planned."

"Good." The knot between my shoulders loosens. "What about the anonymous tip?"

"Happening as we speak." Julia arranged for the desk sergeant to receive new information that one of Joey's fake companies is rumored to have been a cover for money laundering. It might even be true. "That rabbit hole should send them spinning for a long, long time."

Weeks of tension evaporate, and I let out a long, satisfied breath. It's over. No court. No ugly divorce. No husband. I might never have another man who caters to me the way Joey did, who makes me feel like a queen, and that makes me sad. But his betrayal only showed me that, while he might have known how to treat women, he didn't understand us at our core.

The female bond of friendship is not to be taken lightly. We disappoint each other. We might even hurt each other at times, but in the end, we're there for each other, above any man.

Katherine, Julia, Lila, and I have our own private beach club now, born out of love and fed on revenge. The best part is that it comes with a lifetime membership. Now *that's* unbreakable.

House Arrest

By Kathryn Prater Bomey

Suzannah Peters pointed her phone at the wide base of an oak and panned upward. The tree's leafy crown shaded the colonial-style brick home behind it.

"As soon as I saw this beautiful old oak," she said, "I knew this was the house for me."

"Once Lola's big enough," her mother replied on speakerphone, "she'll love playing underneath that tree."

The warm June breeze kicked up, rustling loose a twig that tumbled out of the oak and thwacked a wooden "For Sale" sign.

"Someone needs to nail a 'Sold' badge over that," Suzannah's mom said. "When are you doing the paperwork?"

"I'm meeting the Morales family—the owners—tomorrow."

A cry erupted from a stroller on the sidewalk.

"Let me see that precious girl."

Suzannah angled the phone so her mother and six-month-old daughter could see each other. Her mom cooed, quieting Lola's wails.

She turned the phone back toward herself and smiled at the face on the screen. Suzannah's long, straight brown hair and bangs mirrored her mother's, and she hoped one day Lola's would, too.

"I can't wait to come visit you in your first home," her mom said. "I'm so happy for you and Lola."

"It's all thanks to you," Suzannah said. "Without your help, I couldn't have afforded the down payment—not on my salary. And I wouldn't have been able to pounce on this house before K&M Properties snatched it up."

She angled the camera toward the cookie-cutter house across the street. Brand new, three stories, four thousand square feet. Beige. Bland. Plain siding. Lots of glass. Just like the one to its right. And to *its* right. And as far as the eye could see.

Suzannah sighed. "Mine might be the last colonial—and the last oak tree—standing after K&M gets done with this neighborhood. Did you know they had the nerve to call their new development the Grove? Grove of what? Stumps?"

"Such a shame." Her mom shook her head. "So, when do I get a peek inside your new home?"

"How about right now? I'll hold the phone up to the living room window." Suzannah pushed the stroller up the front walk. A few feet from the house, she slowed.

"Is something wrong?"

"Remember the picture I texted you this morning, during the tour with my real-estate agent? There was a gorgeous wood carving of an oak tree on a table in the living room. But now it's gone."

"Seems too soon for the seller to take down the staging furniture."

"I agree." Still holding the phone, Suzannah marched up to the window. Inside, the living room was a mess. Furniture askew. Objects scattered all over the carpet.

Her hand—and the phone in it—began to shake.

"What's going on?" came her mother's alarmed voice. "Hold the phone still. Is that a—is that a man lying on the floor?"

Suzannah opened her mouth, but her throat was as dry and rough as the bark of the oak tree behind her. Nothing came out but a rasp.

"You've got to help him," her mother said.

She sprinted to the front door and jiggled the knob, but the real-estate agent's lockbox only banged against the wood. The door didn't budge.

Suzannah jabbed the doorbell, then returned to the window and rapped loudly on the glass. The man didn't flinch.

"Mom, I gotta go. I have to call 911."

"Then see if your new neighbor has a spare key or something heavy to break down the door. Maybe you can get in there before it's too late."

A few minutes later, Suzannah was hustling Lola's stroller down the sidewalk next to Greg Chang, the middle-aged man who answered her knock at the house next door.

"I'm a nurse," Suzannah explained. "If he had a heart attack, there might be something I can do before the ambulance gets here."

"I sure hope this works," Greg said, veering toward the garage attached to Suzannah's future home.

She eyed the foot-long hand hoe gripped in his palm. "If it was me, I'd pick a less wimpy tool for knocking down the door."

"No need to knock anything down." Kneeling, he wrapped his fingers underneath the garage door and pulled upward. As he strained, beads of sweat broke out on his forehead. The door lifted one inch, then another.

Greg wedged the miniature hoe underneath, propping the garage door open a foot off the ground.

Panting, he rested his hands on his thighs and gulped in air. "Rick always made that look so easy." He stretched out on his back on the concrete, his short black hair shimmering with sweat.

"Why would Rick break into his own garage?" Suzannah asked.

"Every time Cami kicked him out, she latched the chain lock on the front door."

"But there's a sliding door in the back of the house. I saw it during my tour."

"Cami would jam a broken broom handle into the track at the bottom to stop it from opening, so Rick had to get creative to get back inside."

Sucking in his stomach, Greg wriggled through the opening.

"Why would she—?"

But he was already inside the garage. She heard a *click,* and the door rose the rest of the way.

Greg jumped over two small steps in the rear of the garage, threw open the interior door, and dashed into the house.

Suzannah parked the stroller. "First item on our new homeowner to-do list," she whispered, unbuckling the baby and lifting her out, "is install a lock on this entrance. Second item: get a sturdier garage door that's neighbor-proof."

As a nurse, Suzannah relied on humor as a coping mechanism, but as she looked down at her daughter, her chest constricted. There was nothing funny about exposing Lola to whatever had happened to the man inside. But she had to help him—to try, at least.

Taking a deep breath, she wrapped her arms around Lola and entered the house.

She made her way through the kitchen, then the dining area, and stopped at Greg's side when she reached the edge of the living room.

Suzannah had seen her share of traumatic injury victims at work, but something about this particular sight—the man on his back, unmoving—sent a chill from the top of her head down to her toes.

She turned the baby's face away.

"Is that Rick?" she asked gently.

Pressing his lips together, Greg nodded.

Balancing Lola on one hip, Suzannah squatted and felt Rick's neck for a pulse. There was none.

As she pulled her hand away, the man's head lolled, revealing a bloody gash where his disheveled black hair met his forehead.

Greg let out a loud sob, causing Lola to cry.

Suzannah stroked the back of her daughter's head and looked around. If Rick had suffered a heart attack and fallen, there was nothing near the body he could have hit to cause that wound.

"We should call 911," Greg said, running a hand over his face.

"I did, remember? They should be here soon."

On the gray carpet, a ceramic lamp lay beside an overturned ottoman. Flower stems, petals, and shards of glass from a broken vase were scattered everywhere. Books dotted the floor below a bookshelf.

"It looks like there was a fight," Suzannah said. "Could Rick's wife have done this?"

Greg shook his head. "They hated each other, but they never got violent." He sniffled. "Why was Rick here, anyway? He and Cami moved out weeks ago. They're staying in separate apartments now that the divorce has started."

On the carpet, drops of blood extended out from Rick's body. Some of them were tiny—the size of a pencil eraser. Each was accompanied by a larger, triangle-shaped bloodstain. And they weren't just near the body. They snaked across the carpet along the front of the room, almost like a trail someone had left behind.

"From the looks of the laceration on his head, I doubt he moved after he hit the floor," Suzannah said. "So what caused those bloodstains?"

"My friend is dead, and that's where your head is at?"

"Sorry." Suzannah's cheeks burned. "I'm a bit of a true crime buff. I get a little carried away."

"Then why are you a nurse and not a cop?"

"Law enforcement seemed too dangerous for a single mom." She glanced down at Rick's body. "Apparently buying a house is just as dangerous." A siren sounded in the distance, and Suzannah pulled Lola closer to her chest. "If it wasn't Cami, what if Rick got in a fight with a burglar? The attacker could still be in the house."

Greg stood up straighter. "You stay here with the baby. I'll check the other rooms." He went into the kitchen and slid a knife from a wooden block on the counter.

The hair on the back of Suzannah's neck stood up. Holding Lola so firmly she whimpered and squirmed, she moved aside, giving Greg—and the knife—wide berth as he marched past them and down the hall.

After a few moments, he returned. "Nobody," he said, dropping the knife back into its slot.

Through the window, red and blue lights flashed, and a sheriff's deputy in a brown uniform jogged toward the front door. But coming in that way would mean stepping all over the trail of blood drops. Waving her free arm to get the deputy's attention, Suzannah motioned for him to enter through the garage.

With the stroller bag sitting open on the dining table and Lola on her lap, Suzannah spooned pureed squash into the baby's mouth. Suzannah's own stomach rumbled as she scraped the last bits from the bottom of the jar. Lola fussed when the spoon clinked the glass.

"Now, now, don't be greedy," she whispered. "At least you got a snack. I, on the other hand, might starve to death. Why hasn't that cop let us leave yet?"

In the kitchen, Greg was perched on a chair that Deputy Tim Walton had dragged over so that he and Suzannah wouldn't be close enough to influence each other's stories.

"Where's your backup?" demanded Suzannah. "A 911 call for a dead body in a possible robbery should warrant more than just one responding officer."

Deputy Walton sighed. "We're a small department. A *very* small department."

"You need more manpower. This area isn't as rural as it used to be, with K&M Properties buying our land for cheap and building gigantic housing developments on it," Suzannah said. "Lots of people are moving here from the city."

"You're right, and it's already stretching us thin. We've only got one other officer and one CSI guy, and right now they're both tied up at a different scene clear across the county. Since Mr. Morales is already dead, the EMTs aren't going to rush over from the other call. So it's just me for now."

"If it means we can get out of here sooner, let me help you." Suzannah pulled her phone from her jeans pocket. "I'll send you the photos I took during my tour of the house this morning. You can compare them with the mess in the living room to see what was stolen."

After she texted him the images, Deputy Walton held one of them up and studied it. "Neither of you touched the body, right?"

"Just to check his pulse," Suzannah said.

Walton's eyes widened. "You walked through the crime scene?"

"I didn't touch anything else."

The deputy ran his palm over his close-cropped sandy hair. "I'd like to ask each of you to remove your shoes and set them next to you."

"Why?"

"It doesn't matter why. Just do it."

Suzannah frowned. "You don't have to be so rude. I'm trying to help you, remember?"

Deputy Walton held up his hands. "You're right. But I've got to follow proper protocol. We don't work a lot of crime scenes, which means it's easy to forget things. A mistake today would be my third strike, so I've got to be careful, especially with suspects."

"Excuse me? Suspects?" Suzannah said, her words rising in pitch. Lola, whose eyes had finally closed, now stirred, so Suzannah pushed back the indignation creeping into her voice. "But I'm the one who found him and called 911," she said more softly, stroking the back of the baby's head.

"Wouldn't be the first time a guilty person left and came back to the scene of a crime. Shoes, please."

Suzannah scoffed but complied. As Deputy Walton knelt to photograph her sneakers, she said, "Let me guess: you're going to match photos of our shoes with footprints in the house to make sure our stories line up, right?"

He handed her sneakers back. "No blood on these. At least you were careful when traipsing through my scene. Stay here while I take the rest of my photos. Remember—no talking."

As he captured images of the body, broken glass, and haphazard items scattered across the carpet, Suzannah glanced down and brushed a wisp of brown hair off Lola's forehead. "If I go through with the sale and you grow up here, you're not allowed to remember any of this," she murmured. "Deal?"

In the living room, the deputy bent to take a close-up of a piece of wood lying between Rick and the wall. The oak carving.

Suzannah sprang to her feet. "I know what that is."

When she took a step forward, Walton put up his hand. "Please," he said, "don't walk through here again."

Heat rose to her face, but she ignored it. "During my tour this morning, that carving was right there." She pointed at the table under the window. "If it fell during the burglary, why would it be so far away from the table?"

"It didn't just fall." Grim-faced, Walton turned his phone toward Suzannah. In the photo on the screen, a crimson smear obscured the delicately carved leaves of the miniature tree. "It might have been the murder weapon."

From her seat in the dining room, Suzannah stared at the front door, which she knew was firmly secured on the exterior by the lockbox. The chain lock that Cami had always used against Rick dangled from the wall next to the door. Suzannah twisted in her chair, her eyes wandering to the sliding glass door behind her. Sure enough, half a broom handle was wedged into the track, just as Greg had said.

"Teaching you how to break into the garage was kind of like Rick's way of giving you a spare key, wasn't it?" she called to Greg, who was still in the kitchen. A sense of unease bubbled in her stomach. "So with the front and back doors locked, you were the only one who knew another way in."

"I guess so."

"Why did Rick even need that garage-door workaround, though? Why didn't he just use the keypad to open the garage?"

"Cami changed the code every month."

"Why?"

"She wanted him to sit outside—the more miserable the weather, the better—and think about what he'd done."

"What *did* he do?"

"He slid in under the door."

"No, I mean, what did he do to make her so mad?"

Deputy Walton walked into the kitchen, his hands on his hips. "I told you to stop talking. If my colleague was here, we'd put you in separate squad cars, but right now, this is the best I can do. Please cooperate."

Greg looked chastised, and Suzannah dipped her chin to the top of her daughter's head and inhaled the scent of baby shampoo. Instead of calming her, it only reminded her how vulnerable Lola was.

Muffled voices came from the porch, and there were two *clicks* as the lockbox snapped open and shut. A key scraped, and the front door began to swing—right into the crime scene.

"Stop right there," Deputy Walton commanded. When the door kept moving, he tried again, louder. "*Stop!*"

That time, it worked.

"You don't have to shout," said a woman from outside. A business card slithered around the edge of the door. "Eliza King, real-estate agent. I'm here with the owner."

Suzannah's eyes dropped to the body on the floor. "Uh, we're looking at the owner right now," she said, "and he's sure not standing out there with you."

"Rick?" came a different female voice. "Rick, are you in there?"

The card disappeared, and the door started to move again.

"Don't open that," Walton said. "You'll disturb the crime scene."

"Crime scene?" said the second woman. "What's going on? Is my husband there? I'm coming in through the garage."

The two women hurried across the yard past the living room window. High-heeled footsteps clacked on the garage concrete, then the kitchen tile.

Eliza, still clutching her business card and dressed in a skirt suit and stilettos, marched in first, followed by Cami in a floral sundress and flats. They both halted at the sight of the body on the floor, the color draining from their faces.

Cami's hand flew to her mouth. "Rick? Is he—"

"He's gone." Greg threw his arms around her. "I'm so sorry, Cami."

She stiffened. "Get off me," she said, shrugging her shoulders so forcefully that he couldn't hold on.

He stumbled backward. "Aren't you upset?"

"Why should I be? This works out better than the divorce—I'll get to keep everything now, instead of half."

Greg blinked several times, then shook his head. He turned to Eliza. "I saw you here earlier today, when I was mowing my lawn."

"This house is my listing. I have a right to be here. And there was a tour for a prospective buyer."

"Yeah, but you weren't here for it," Suzannah chimed in. "I'm the buyer, and it was just my agent and me this morning. So why were you—?"

"You're going to make me put in new carpet, aren't you?" Cami interrupted, turning to her.

"Well, someone has to replace it," Suzannah said. "There's blood everywhere."

"The dots are only on the far side of the room. So I only need to replace half, starting right about—"

"Mrs. Morales, get back in the kitchen, please. You're contaminating the crime scene." Deputy Walton's voice was firm. "*Now.*"

Cami pulled her foot back. "But it's my house."

"Doesn't matter," Walton said.

Suzannah looked down at her daughter, then lifted her head. "You may not need to worry about the carpet on my account, Cami. I'm considering rescinding my offer."

"You can't pull out," Cami said, the volume of her voice escalating. "We had a deal."

Lola let out a wail.

Suzannah glared at Cami and patted Lola's back. "I haven't signed anything. Just a verbal agreement over the phone, remember? That's not binding. Maybe your agent should have shown up for the tour. Then we might have gotten some of the paperwork done."

Cami scowled at Eliza.

"Don't look at *me*," Eliza said. "You're the one who wanted to sell as fast as possible, so Rick's brother wouldn't find out this place was on the market. Your spite is what made the deal sloppy."

As tears streamed down Lola's puffy face, Suzannah bounced the baby on her hip.

"Who can blame her for getting cold feet?" Eliza said. "Look at that sweet child. Suzannah just wants to keep her safe." She crossed her arms and tapped the tip of her stiletto on the kitchen tile. "We have other options, Cami. Remember, K&M made a very attractive offer."

"K&M?" Suzannah said. "The only reason that company would buy this house is to tear it down, just like they've done to so many other beautiful old colonials in the neighborhood."

Cami threw up her hands. "Eliza, I've told you again and again—I'm not selling to my brother-in-law. I won't give that family the satisfaction."

Suzannah's ears pricked up. "Rick's brother owns K&M Properties?"

"Co-owns. And I can't wait to sever ties with that family, as soon as the divorce is final." With a glance at Rick's body, she smirked. "Actually, I guess I don't have to wait."

"If the M in K&M is for Morales, what's the K stand for?" Deputy Walton asked.

Suzannah slid out her phone and flipped to the photos she'd taken for her mom earlier that day. She zoomed in on the K&M welcome sign that hung at the entrance to the Grove.

"King," she read from the picture. She locked eyes with Eliza. "Isn't that your last name?"

"A lot of people around here have that last name. The King family's been a mainstay of this community for generations."

"Eliza's gaslighting you," Cami said. "Her brother is business partners with Rick's brother. Our families have been close for years. A King brother and a Morales brother—together, they own K&M Properties." She cocked her head. "Owned, I mean."

"Ms. King," Deputy Walton said, "Greg saw you on the premises today, and it wasn't for a tour. Why were you here?"

"I know why," Suzannah said, her pulse speeding up. "She came after I left, entered using the key in the lockbox, and ransacked the living room." She turned to Eliza. "You wanted to make it look like a dangerous neighborhood to scare the buyer—me—off."

Cami's mouth dropped open. "Did you think losing this sale would make me desperate enough to sell to K&M? Did they offer you some kind of deal—a cut of the profits from the new house K&M would build after demolishing this one?"

"You're my client," Eliza said, backing into the kitchen. "I was simply trying to get you the best possible outcome." She grabbed a knife—the one Greg had returned—from the block on the counter and held it in front of her, pointing the tip at them.

Suzannah's heart slammed against her chest.

"Easy with that," Deputy Walton said, taking a step toward Eliza. His hand was poised over the gun holstered on his belt.

"I bet Rick forgot something," Suzannah went on, "snuck in through the garage to get it, and caught you staging the burglary." She managed to keep her voice steady as she tried not to stare at the knife—or the deputy's gun.

Eliza backed up a pace. Then another.

"But why kill him?" Suzannah asked, trying to pull Eliza's eyes toward her as Walton advanced. "If your brother co-owned the development company, wouldn't Rick have been on board with your plan?"

Knuckles white around the grip of the knife, Eliza took two more steps back, arriving at the door to the garage.

"I didn't know who it was," Eliza said. "He snuck up behind me. But I knew somebody was there, because I heard the crunch when he stepped on a piece of glass. I was about to put the oak carving on the floor, to make it look like it'd been knocked down in the burglary."

Suzannah glimpsed movement in her peripheral vision, but she didn't turn to look. When the front door creaked, she held her eye contact with Eliza, hoping she wouldn't notice.

"So you swung the carving and hit Rick in the head," Suzannah said. "You might have gotten away with claiming it was a random burglary, if Greg hadn't seen you." She pointed at Eliza's feet. "And if you hadn't missed a spot." A smudge of crimson peeked out from the sole of Eliza's stiletto. "Those bloodstains on the carpet were from your high heels. You walked away from Rick's dead body and left through the front door like nothing had happened."

Eliza raised the knife. Suzannah held her breath and wrapped her body around Lola as a shield.

With her other hand, Eliza pushed open the kitchen door behind her. Still facing them, she stepped backward down the two stairs that led into the garage, which was open to the outside as Suzannah and Greg had left it.

Then, the garage-door motor roared to life, sawing through the tense silence as the door began to lower.

As her escape route shrank, panic streaked across Eliza's face. Dropping the knife, she spun and bolted, with Deputy Walton close behind.

But the garage door was fully closed now, and Eliza's shoulders sagged as Walton unhooked a pair of handcuffs from his belt and snapped them on her wrists.

Greg, who must have been the one Suzannah heard sneaking out of the house moments before, stood beside the door that connected the kitchen and garage, his hand still poised above the button that had activated the garage door. In her panic, Eliza had run right past him.

"With all this breaking and entering and sneaking around, I can't decide whether he's a creepy neighbor or a resourceful one," Suzannah whispered to Lola. "What do you think?" The baby reached up and swatted Suzannah's chin. "Yeah, I'm leaning toward resourceful, too."

Cami pinched the bridge of her nose with her thumb and index fingers and closed her eyes, as if battling a sudden migraine. "Okay," she said, dropping her hand from her face, "I'll replace the carpet." She narrowed her eyes in Greg's direction. "And the garage door." She turned to Suzannah. "And anything else. Name it. I just want to get far away from the King and Morales families and K&M Properties. You've got to take this house off my hands. I'm begging you."

Suzannah glanced down at Lola and grinned. "Looks like we're going to get our beautiful oak tree, after all."

Who Killed Mother Theresa

By Maggie King

"My dear Ashley, I'm *so* sorry for your loss. I'll never, *ever*, get over finding your mother like that." The fragile-looking woman gripped my hand with surprising strength. Her dark, birdlike eyes filled with tears.

"Oh, you must be Mom's cleaner," I said. "I heard you found her. That must have been awful for you."

"Your mother was such a wonderful woman. I'd only been cleaning for her for a few months, but she quickly became my favorite client."

I shook my head, trying to erase the vision of the woman before me arriving at my mother's house for her weekly cleaning, only to find Mom in bed with a long magenta scarf wrapped tightly around her neck. The scarf I'd given her for Christmas months before.

Mom and I had shared a love of TV murder mysteries, and we often rolled our eyes at the frequency of cleaners finding their clients dead.

Mom, you got caught in a cliché.

The woman—what did she say her name was?—continued to grip my hand as she nattered on. She had to practically crane her neck at a ninety-degree angle to look up at me. Finally, she gave my hand a pat before letting the next person in line offer condolences. A seemingly endless parade of mourners hugged me and asked if there was anything they could do to help. "Thank you," I murmured to each person in turn. Some I knew, some I didn't. A good number were associated with RiseUp, a non-profit devoted to helping the homeless get back on their feet. Mom had served as CEO for the past five years.

"You look so much like your dear mother, with those lovely blue eyes." The complimentary woman was another hand gripper. She didn't comment on my purple-streaked blond hair or the various flowers inked on my arms, but her raised eyebrows made her thoughts clear.

Finally, the line ended and my friend Hailey appeared at my side, a glass of wine in each hand.

"Thanks, I need this." I took the glass she thrust at me and sipped. Mom's funeral lunch was held at Grace of the Redeemer Church, perched on a bluff overlooking the James River in Richmond. The floor-to-ceiling glass walls of the fellowship hall offered a stunning view of the river.

"Let's look at the video," I said. "I haven't had a chance to see how the funeral director put it together."

A video loop displayed images of Teresa Pinnick as a babe in arms, as a toddler splashing in a wading pool, as a graduate from various institutions, as a bride to two different husbands, and with me at various ages. A recent photo showed her with a group from RiseUp. Scrapbooks, framed photos, and arrangements of yellow roses covered a nearby table.

"Come on, Ashley. Let's get something to eat," Hailey said after two loops.

The deli platters, salads, and desserts that filled a long table by one of the glass walls didn't appeal to me. While Hailey filled a plate, I chatted with a few of Mom's friends.

"This is some turnout," Hailey said, returning with what looked like a sample of every item from the table. "Eight eulogies! Yours was the best."

"I thought that guy RiseUp helped get back on track was the best. He's in law school now."

"Why didn't your mom's husband say something? I know they were separated, but still."

I made a face. "I'd be happier if Danny hadn't shown up at all."

Danny Arnold, a tall man in a well-tailored suit, stood by a glass wall. All dimples and white teeth, he held a group of women in thrall.

"That's quite a blondetourage he has over there," Hailey said.

I turned my attention from Danny and his groupies to the rest of the crowd. "If I find the scumbag who killed my mom, he—or she—will have hell to pay."

"Have you talked to the police?" Hailey tucked a strand of black hair behind an ear.

"Many times, but they're not about to share their progress with me. Assuming they've made any. One of the detectives working the case is here, observing everyone while shoveling food in his mouth." I used my glass to point to a stocky figure by the food table. "I hope he's keeping Danny in his sights. I sure am."

Hailey's eyes opened wide. "You really think—"

"Yeah, I really think. Danny's a slick one. Never trusted him. Besides, in mysteries the police always suspect the spouse, especially when money's involved. That woman Danny left Mom for might have put him up to it. He stands to get a fortune—unless Mom changed her will. I sure hope she did. I should tell him what I think."

"That's not a good idea," Hailey said, a warning in her voice. She knew how headstrong and impulsive I could be. "Let the police find who killed your mom."

A burst of laughter came from the women circling Danny. "Mr. Charming," I said. I stuck my finger in my mouth, miming retching.

"Is she here?" Hailey asked. "His girlfriend?"

I shook my head. "I don't think so. Mom said her name's Sandy, and I haven't met anyone with that name."

"Probably didn't have the nerve to show up," Hailey said.

I took my phone from my purse. "Let me show you this picture. I haven't seen anyone who looks—"

"Ms. Ashley? May I say how very sorry I am about your mother's passing."

A thirtysomething man with intense hazel eyes and a blond ponytail trailing down his back loomed before me. He intoned like an undertaker—in fact, more like an undertaker than the one who'd handled Mom's funeral arrangements. He wasn't the best dresser, wearing ill-fitting slacks paired with a corduroy jacket that had either come from a thrift store or should be headed to one.

"Passing?" I snorted. "You mean murder." I put the phone back in my purse.

"Yes, well."

"And you are?"

"Jake Patrick. Call me Jake. I'm the Community Coordinator with RiseUp. I very much admired your mother." Jake smiled at Hailey. "Have we met before?"

"Yes, two weeks ago at La Trattoria. You were with Ashley's mom."

"Ah, yes." Jake reddened.

What's this all about? I wondered.

Hailey tried to split a meatball with a plastic fork. When the meatball vaulted off her plate and wound up impaled by a woman's stiletto, Jake rushed for napkins and cleaned up the mess. The three of us shared a laugh.

Still laughing, I checked the time on my phone. "Gotta dash. The lawyer's reading the will at two. Hailey, walk me to my car." I turned to Jake. "Nice meeting you."

Outside, a gentle May breeze stirred the leaves of the trees. Hailey and I stopped by two enormous rhododendron bushes, pink blossoms big as platters. "What was that about my mom and Jake?"

"I saw them at La Trattoria," Hailey said. "Your mom introduced him as her colleague, but they looked pretty cozy for colleagues, sitting close together. They weren't thrilled to see me."

"Hmmph. Well, she didn't share that with me. Why didn't you?"

"Work's been so busy, I forgot about it 'til now. Sorry about that."

"I guess Jake goes on the suspect list as well."

"Why?"

"Why not? Maybe he has a record. Maybe she found out something about him. Maybe she spurned him. Maybe he's a psychopath."

At Hailey's alarmed look, I held up my hand. "I know, I know, I'm reaching."

"I'm sure your mom did background checks on prospective employees. She must have thought he was a safe bet."

My eyes filled with tears. Hailey put her arm around me and pulled me close. "Ashley, the police will find who killed her."

After promising to get together before returning home to New York, I clicked my key fob to open my car door.

"What were you going to show me on your phone?" Hailey asked.

"Oh! I'll show you later. I'm running late."

When I started the engine, I spotted Danny emerging from the church, his gaggle of blondes in tow.

I fantasized about running over the lot of them.

My mother's will read, Danny and I stood. I thanked the lawyer, and Danny stormed out of the office. I caught him by the elevator, stabbing the down button. He scowled at me but said nothing. Our silence continued in the elevator and through the lobby, elegant with abstract paintings and well-cared-for plants. In the parking lot, Danny continued to ignore me.

"Not so fast, Danny," I said, as he opened his Acura's door. "We need to talk."

The man shot me a look of pure hatred, but I willed myself not to flinch.

A woman clutching an oversized phone emerged from the car. Blond waves brushed her shoulders. Cleavage spilled over the neckline of a ruffled black blouse. One of Danny's admirers from the church.

"Sandy! Get back in the car." Danny sounded like he was dealing with an unruly five-year-old.

Sandy? This was Sandy?

The woman ignored him and fixed her gaze on me.

Danny turned to me and sputtered. "I guess you're happy, getting all that money."

"Oh, no." Sandy brought a hand to her lips, fingers festooned with rings and blood-red talons.

"Yeah, I'm pretty happy," I said. "All that money *and* the house. Of course, RiseUp and a couple of other charities got a good chunk of Mom's fortune. My grandfather's fortune, rather. But what makes me happiest, Danny, is that you got nothing. *Nada.* You killed Mom for nothing."

Sandy gasped, while Danny advanced on me. "Now you listen to me, you little bitch," he said, shaking his finger. "That's slander."

I didn't move a muscle. "Get your finger out of my face. You killed Mom, and I'm going to prove it. You don't deserve any of her money."

"I'm afraid I do, my dear." Danny lowered his finger and stepped back.

"Don't *my dear* me."

"Teresa was my lawfully wedded wife."

Busy Patterson Avenue wasn't the best place for this showdown, but in light of my suspicions about my stepfather, it was probably the safest. Surely, a passing driver would see any questionable activity and call the police. I hoped.

"Oh, please. If you and your son hadn't been selling hot appliances online, Mom wouldn't have thrown you out. You're lucky she didn't report you." At Sandy's surprised look, I said, "He didn't tell you about his little business venture, did he?"

I reached into my purse. Suddenly, the two looked nervous. "Don't worry, I don't have a gun, and if I did, I wouldn't use it here in broad daylight."

I produced my phone and opened my photos app. "The last time I visited Mom, we looked through her photo albums, and I digitized this one." I held up a picture of a smiling couple. A banner with the words "Congratulations on your engagement!" spanned a wall behind a table decorated with balloons and a huge chocolate sheet cake. "The man is clearly my dad, but who was this woman? Mom explained that she was Sandy Schuller, dad's former fiance. Things didn't work out with them."

"She stole him from me!" Sandy's kohl-lined eyes blazed. A breeze stirred, setting her silver earrings tinkling like wind chimes.

"So this *is* you." The woman in the picture had chin-length chestnut hair, blue eyes, and the kind of wholesome beauty that graced the covers of teen fashion magazines. "You look very, um, *different* these days. But, after all, this happy occasion was over thirty years ago."

Sandy folded her arms, lifting the cleavage, making it look even more combustible.

"Mom said you and she were friends. Is that right?"

"*Were* friends. Until she stole my fiancé."

"So you've said. Maybe Dad just decided he preferred Mom. It happens. I did some Googling. You and Mom both went to college here in Richmond and became social workers. Dad was a med student. You and he became engaged, but as Mom said, it didn't work out. I bet you felt smug when their marriage didn't last."

"I felt lucky. He turned out to be gay."

Danny huffed an explosive sigh. "Is there a point to all this, Ashley?"

I glared at him. "Good old Google came up with more interesting information: you finally managed to snag a husband, Sandy, but he died three years ago. You were still angry at Mom, so you decided to steal *her* husband." I waved a hand at Danny. "Such a prize."

"You stole me from my wife?" Danny cast an admiring look at Sandy. Did he actually puff himself up, or was that my imagination?

Sandy tried, and failed, to assume an innocent air. "I didn't realize you were married to Teresa. I was amazed when I found out you were."

I laughed. "Oh, Danny. If you believe that crap, you're dumber than I thought—if that's even possible. Sandy didn't steal you. Mom had already thrown you out. True, you and Mom were still married, and Sandy may not have known you were camping out on Danny Jr.'s sofa. So if it makes you both feel better, Sandy can claim to be a husband stealer."

Danny leaned against the car and shook his head.

"As for you, Ms. Sandy, I'd think you were innocent in all this, but—"

"Oh, so you think I murdered your dear sweet mom. Well, you can just look elsewhere, Ashley Pinnick. You'll find scores of others with motives for killing her."

"Like who? Mom was a wonderful person. She helped the homeless get back on their feet. She supported the food bank."

"Yeah, she was a do-gooder, but she made plenty of enemies before she became *Mother* Teresa. She didn't limit her sins to stealing fiancés and boyfriends. In high school, she was quite the bully. She really picked on the nerdy guys. Then there was—" Sandy stopped, looking unsure about finishing her sentence.

"Go on," I said with an impatient wave of my hand.

"—Freda Davies. She was really mean to her. But Freda's dead, so she couldn't be the culprit."

"What did Mom do to Freda?" Did I really want to know this stuff about my mother? But something drove me to ask.

"Freda was a nerdy sort, socially awkward, and Teresa teased her mercilessly. Teresa had this entourage of guys who doted on her, obeyed her every command. She got one of her lap dogs to feign interest in Freda. Of course, Freda was flattered, and one night she went to the guy's house when his parents were away, and they got into a compromising situation. Teresa burst into the bedroom and started snapping pictures. Freda, as you can imagine, was mortified and humiliated. I'm sure you can guess what came next. Teresa passed the pictures around at school. What might surprise you is what Freda did: one day in English class, as the pictures made the rounds, Freda up and beat the crap out of Teresa. Black eye, split lip, you name it. Both girls were suspended, and Freda never returned to school. Your grandfather stormed over to Freda's and confronted her mom. The two had a screaming match, but neither pressed charges. Teresa was pretty upset with her father about that."

"When did Mom change?" I asked. "Become, well, *nice*."

"It started in college. I can't tell you what prompted it, but it was a slow change, since she stole your dad from me."

I ignored the repeated reference to the fiancé theft. "When did Freda die?"

"About a year ago, maybe two. Suicide. She was a longtime member of a support group that my colleague led. It seems Freda hung onto her grudge against Teresa, even after more than thirty years. She never got over the humiliation."

"Really? People hold grudges for that long?"

"Some do. The damages from cruelties suffered in childhood can last a lifetime."

"Spoken like a true social worker," I said, with a sort of laugh. "What about the guy, the so-called lap dog? Didn't Freda hold a grudge against him?"

"I don't think so. She probably knew Teresa had put him up to it."

"If Mom was so horrible, why were you friends with her?"

Sandy studied her strappy black sandals, as if she hoped they'd give her an answer. "Um, it was…safer that way." I wondered if she was about to expose a vulnerable side. Her lifting her chin in a show of defiance dashed that expectation. "So there you have it."

Danny looked as stunned as I felt. Mom a mean girl?

In the TV murder mysteries Mom and I watched, often the killer was seeking revenge for the murder of a family member. "Maybe Freda's mother killed my mom," I said.

"She'd be pretty old by now. I don't even know if she's still around." Sandy managed a sad little smile. "Look, Ashley, Danny and I are very sorry about your mom. But we didn't have anything to do with her death. If you want to play detective, start here." She rattled off four names that I prayed would stick with me.

"I don't know, Sandy. I think you're trying to sidetrack me." I turned to Danny. "I happen to know that once Grandpa's will went through probate, you begged Mom to take you back. You even promised to keep your business dealings legitimate. But Mom refused. She'd had enough of you. She was about to file for divorce."

"What! You *begged* her to take you back?" Sandy shrieked. Her nose flared, and her eyes widened.

Danny looked alarmed. "She's lying."

"You know I'm not," I said. "You just wanted to get your hands on that money. You didn't know if she'd changed her will. Maybe you checked the safe deposit box and found that she hadn't. But you didn't know if she *would* change it, so you had to kill her before she got around to it. Turns out that she did change it and had the new will notarized. She just hadn't gotten to the bank yet."

Danny gritted his pretty white teeth. "Now, wait a minute. Sandy and I were in Nag's Head the night Teresa was killed." He looked at Sandy for support, but she was stabbing at her phone. Red lips flattened into a narrow line. "And how would we get in the house, anyway? She changed the locks the day I moved out."

"There are probably other ways in. Or maybe she *let* you in. Nags Head isn't that far away, three hours or so. You could have driven here and back. I bet no one can verify your alibi."

"The police were satisfied," Danny said. "If you're not, you'll need to come up with some proof." He opened the driver's side door and turned to me. "As I recall, you and your mother weren't on the best of terms."

"We'd reconciled."

"When, after your dear grandpa died?"

"What are you implying?"

"Nothing. Just stating facts." His smile didn't reach his eyes. "Have you considered your mother's cleaner? She probably had a key."

"The cleaner? That's ridiculous. Why would she kill Mom?"

A car pulled into the lot and stopped. Sandy checked the license plate, then opened the rear passenger door.

"Where are you going?" Danny sputtered.

"Home. You can come by and get your things. You tried to go back with your wife, and you probably killed her. We're through." She slid into the back seat of the car, and the driver—Uber, I presumed—took off.

Danny got in his car and peeled out of the lot, following Sandy.

Did that spell curtains for their relationship? Probably. But if Danny had benefited from my mother's will, I bet Sandy would have stayed with him, despite any qualms about his illegal activities or questionable fidelity.

I remembered two of the names of victims of my mother's alleged bullying and texted them to myself. Pretty good, with my being so bad with names.

I was determined to find Mom's killer. The police weren't getting anywhere, at least not fast enough to suit me. I still pegged Danny as the culprit. And there was Jake—but I had nothing concrete on him. I'd see what I could unearth with these names.

Back at my mother's house—my house now—I knew I couldn't stay. The specter of Danny and Sandy managing to break in and kill me wouldn't be conducive to sleeping. After arranging to spend the night with Hailey, I gathered Mom's photo albums and Fredericksburg High School yearbooks. The police still had her phone, laptop, and iPad.

Hailey lived in a duplex in the Fan, a historic section of Richmond known for its restaurants, nightlife, and post-Victorian architecture. As I wheeled my luggage along Hailey's street, I admired the charming homes with their bay windows, stained glass, and turrets.

While Hailey and I waited for a pizza delivery, I pored over the yearbooks. Mom—then Teresa Simpson—had that confident look reserved for the cheerleaders and cool crowd that populated every high school. Both girls Sandy had named came right out of central casting for Geek: thick, black-framed glasses and greasy strands of hair trailing down their foreheads. As for Freda Davies, a mottled complexion suggested that acne added to her adolescent suffering.

One by one, I Googled the names. One was now a state senator in Pennsylvania, the other CEO of a telecommunications firm in Northern Virginia. Apparently, these leaders had transcended their less-than-stellar high-school experiences.

Freda Davies hadn't fared as well. I sipped my wine as I read her obit. Freda, a sales associate at Walmart, had died in April of the previous year, a year to the day before Mom died.

A year to the day.

A chill went through me. I was glad Hailey was in the next room.

Freda's mother had pre-deceased her. That left her out of the suspect pool, even if she'd been strong enough to kill. Freda's sole survivor was a sister, Linda Stefanik.

I Googled Linda Stefanik and clicked on one of those sites that offer information about people: birth date, places lived, politics, religion, income. "Also known as" caught my attention—Linda Stefanik was also known as Linda Deale.

Linda Deale. Where had I heard that name?

Back to Google. Linda Deale owned a local cleaning service. I gasped at the picture of the strong, confident woman who smiled from my screen. But she was definitely the same tiny, birdlike woman I'd met earlier, who'd patted my hand and been so grief-stricken over losing her favorite client. Her words—"It was so awful to find your mother like that"—rang in my ears. Also: "I'd only been cleaning for her for a few months."

Tears ran down my face as I pictured Mom with that beautiful magenta scarf circling her neck. Did Linda Deale kill my mother to avenge her sister's suicide on the anniversary of her death? Sure looked like it. But I was done playing detective. I would report what I knew to the police, and let them take it from here.

So, Danny and Sandy, I guess you two are off the hook now.

Bad Date Rescue

By Adam Meyer

Maggie stood at the mirror in the too-bright bathroom, checking her makeup, feeling a tingle along the back of her neck like she was being watched. Looking up, she saw another woman's reflection moving in, overlapping hers. Long dark hair around a thin face with high cheekbones. She wore a tight-fitting sweater and jeans molded to her long legs, the kind Maggie had tried on a few times but could never seem to pull off.

"You on a first date?" the woman asked.

Maggie turned from the mirror. "How'd you know?"

The woman smiled, her teeth bright and sharp. "I can tell. Good luck."

Maggie was about to continue the conversation when she felt her phone buzz. Tess, of course. She hit a button to send the call to voicemail, then looked up, but the dark-haired woman was gone.

She made her way back out through the crowded restaurant to the bar. The Dogwood had opened on Charlottesville's Downtown Mall in the spring and had quickly become popular with patrons of all ages. The booths were full of couples on double dates, wedged in side-by-side and sharing colorful drinks. The bar was jammed with college students chugging Starr Hill lagers and passing their phones back and forth. Maggie, who'd worked as an adjunct in the English department at UVA for the last five years, prayed she didn't run into any of her former charges—not tonight.

Squeezing through the throng of young bodies, she spotted Dylan again and felt a faint flutter in her chest.

Almost two years since the end of her last relationship, she couldn't help but wonder: was he *the one*?

Even though he had shown up twenty minutes late—"I'm so sorry! I had to stop to help a friend and my cell was out of juice," he'd said when he first rushed in—he was just as good-looking as in his online photos. That was rare. Sure, the conversation had been a little stiff, and he was fidgety, nervous. But Maggie wasn't going to hold it against him. She hadn't been on a date in a few months herself and had some nerves of her own.

Sliding onto the stool beside him, she forced a smile.

"You're back," Dylan said, taking a sip of beer. "I was afraid you might've run off."

"And why would you think that?"

"Oh, just kidding…but the last couple women I went out with got scared off."

Her stomach clenched. Here it was, the reason Dylan was thirty-five and single. "Scared off by what?"

"Nothing, really. It's just…relationships can be tough, you know."

"Yeah, definitely."

Her cell phone buzzed. Tess again.

NO RESCUE NEEDED? FINGERS CROSSED! DON'T DO ANYTHING I WOULDN'T DO ☺

Maggie glanced at her phone before laying it flat. When she looked up, Dylan was studying her. She flushed, realizing she'd been rude. "Sorry, I—"

Dylan glanced around nervously, then back at her. "No, don't worry about it."

"That was just my friend Tess, checking in on me."

"Making sure I'm not a serial killer?"

"Something like that."

What she didn't say was that Tess was her BDR, or Bad Date Rescue. Every time Maggie went on a date, Tess called after forty minutes, just in case she needed an excuse to get away. If she answered, Tess would tell her there was a family emergency or her dog was sick—not that Maggie even had a pet—and she had to come right home. Maggie had mixed feelings about the ruse, but Tess insisted on it. You never know when a date might really go off the rails, she explained, drawing on her own vast experience with online dating.

Of course, Maggie didn't tell Dylan that. She knew what was and wasn't appropriate—especially on a first date.

"So you said you like to travel." She took another sip of white wine, trying to settle her nerves. "What's the last place you went?"

"Mexico. It was beautiful."

"I've always wanted to go." Maggie leaned in, wondering if her just-slightly-low-cut sweater was showing too much cleavage. "Where in Mexico?"

"Puerto Vallarta. We went because Amanda…." Dylan trailed off, looking down at his beer. "Sorry, never mind."

"No, of course you went with your ex. It's not like we're in high school or something, right? I mean, everybody's got…baggage."

Maggie felt a sudden urge to hide behind the bar. She'd meant *history*, not baggage. As an English teacher, she knew that using the right word was important. All the more so when she was trying to make a good impression on a first date.

"You're right," he said, nodding vigorously. "Everyone does have baggage. Some more than others, I guess."

Maggie frowned. Did he mean *her*? No, he couldn't, he hardly even knew her.

"I'm making a mess of this." Dylan covered his face with his hands, then peered at her through his fingers, looking earnest. "Can we start over?"

"Sure," she said, laughing despite herself.

He put out a hand, touching hers lightly. "I'm Dylan. You must be Maggie."

"I am. It's nice to finally meet you in person."

"Same here. I—"

He glanced across the bar, where a mirror reflected the tables behind them, then took a last sip of his beer, thunked it down, shook his head. "Look, I've made a mistake. A really big mistake."

"You mean what you said before? It's fine, really."

He slid off the stool, shaking his head. "No, not that."

"I don't understand."

He looked her straight in the eye, the first time he'd done so without fidgeting. "I thought it would be a good thing for me to get out there again, and when we met online, I really liked you. But…I shouldn't. I can't. It's not that I'm not over Amanda, my ex-girlfriend—ex-fiancée, really—because I am. It's just…you seem like a nice person, and you deserve better."

"Okay, but we're just having a drink, right? I mean—"

He pulled a rumpled bill from his pocket, dropped it on the bar. "If we'd met some other time, some other place, then maybe.…" He shook his head. "Good night, Maggie."

With that, he was off, making his way through the crowd, heading for the front door.

Maggie had been on some dud first dates, but this was a real Hall of Famer, the kind she and Tess would laugh about someday. Only Maggie didn't feel like laughing. Mostly she wanted to throw up.

Instead, she forced herself to finish her glass of wine and shook her head when the bartender offered another.

Cool air brushed her skin as she headed out onto the Downtown Mall. The brightly lit marquee of the Paramount Theater glowed in the distance. She thought of all the times she'd gone there with her ex to see some old movie or standup act. Wouldn't it be nice to have someone to go out with again, to do the things she loved doing?

She took a deep breath and pulled out her phone. Her first instinct was to call Tess, but she didn't want to, not yet. Instead, she ordered an Uber and saw that her driver, Grant, would arrive in five minutes.

She moved past a group of outdoor tables and headed up Second Street, weaving through packs of drunken students and homeless people. The din from the nearby restaurants and bars was not quite loud enough to muffle the voice in her head. What if she ended up single forever? There was nothing wrong with that, of course, she had lots of friends who were happy on their own. But whenever she looked at Tess—married for almost a year now and trying to get pregnant—she felt a pang of jealousy.

As she came out to Market Street, she checked the curb for her Uber but didn't see it. The app had told her that Grant would be driving a Nissan Sentra—although, truth be told, she couldn't tell one kind of car from another. A short way down the sidewalk, a man paced back and forth, maybe waiting for his own ride. Across the street loomed the Central Library, a couple of young people kissing in the shadow of its columned portico.

She looked away.

"Just stop it, all right!" A man's voice carried on the faint breeze. "This has gone too far, much too far!"

It was the man she'd seen pacing on the sidewalk, and as he moved beneath the glow of a streetlight, she realized it was Dylan. Clearly, he'd been lying when he said he couldn't call to say he was running late because his phone had no power.

She watched him closely, but he was so caught up in his conversation he didn't seem to notice. After a moment he spoke again, more softly, so she couldn't hear what he was saying. Still, he was clearly upset. Not that it mattered. Dylan was history.

A band of frustration tightened across her shoulders. It didn't matter about Dylan, not really. The problem was just knowing that she'd had another missed connection, another night of going home to an empty bed.

Meeeeeep-meeeep!

A curvy black four-door idled at the curb.

The driver looked to be late thirties, hair graying at the temples, dark eyes drilling into hers. He wore a baggy sweatshirt, probably to hide a beer gut, and had a small gap between his top front teeth. "Hey, I've been waiting."

"Sorry, I got distracted." Maggie slipped into the back seat and hunted for the seatbelt. "Long night."

"Tell me about it."

"I said I'm sorry."

He shrugged and turned a knob on the radio. Jazz filled the car, something she recognized but couldn't place, not at first.

"Is that Duke Ellington?" she asked.

"Mingus, actually. From *East Coasting*."

Nodding, she leaned back, let the music wash over her. She'd gone to see a jazz concert at Old Cabbell Hall on campus last year, and while the music was excellent, the guy she'd brought with her had fallen asleep before intermission. Another date gone wrong. Not the first and clearly not the last. She pulled out her phone and texted Tess.

DATE WAS A BUST ☹

She glanced out the window, watching as Grant made a right onto Avon Avenue, heading through Belmont. The houses here were old and narrow, sitting shoulder-to-shoulder like the couples in the booths at the Dogwood earlier.

A buzz from her phone. Tess.

SO SORRY!!! COME BY FOR A DRINK ASAP!!!

Maggie hesitated. She knew that seeing her old grad-school friend would comfort her. Still, the last thing she wanted was to barge in on Tess and Mark on a Friday night. She considered for a moment, then tapped out her reply.

THANKS BUT NOT TONIGHT

Looking up from her phone, she saw the sidewalks fall away, the houses spaced more widely apart and set further back from the road. A full moon rose above, hanging like a beachball in the vast night sky.

JUST HANG IN THERE—YOU'LL MEET SOMEONE!!

Tess's optimism caught Maggie off-guard. Looking on the sunny side wasn't her usual style. Maybe she'd gotten good news from the fertility doctor?

"Sheesh, some people just don't know how to drive."

She had nearly forgotten about Grant, who was growling at his rearview mirror. Turning, she saw a pair of headlights, close enough to blind her.

"What's going on?" she asked.

"Nothing, just some guy in a hurry. He'll probably turn off at Fifth Street Station, must be late for a movie or something." He glanced at the rearview, though Maggie wasn't sure if he was studying her or the road. "You on your way home from a date?"

Maggie bristled. "That's none of your business."

"I'll take that as a yes. Seems kind of early."

"I was just meeting an old friend for a drink."

"If you say so. I don't know about you, but I stay off those dating apps, never meet anyone good that way."

"Mmmm," Maggie said, looking down at her phone to make it clear that the conversation was over. How had things gotten to the point where even her Uber driver was weighing in on her love life?

Looking over, she saw that they had just driven past the entrance to Fifth Street Station. Behind her, the headlights were still blindingly bright and closer than she would've liked. She leaned toward Grant. "Maybe we could pull over somewhere and let them pass us?"

"Pull over where? Nothing ahead, except for the jail."

That wasn't quite true. There was an elementary school about a mile ahead on the left and a strip mall just past that. But Maggie took the driver's point: Avon Street was one lane in either direction with no passing. The car behind them ought to simply back off until the road ahead opened up.

She looked at her phone, wondering if she ought to reconsider Tess's offer. She could go home, take off her date clothes and slip into something way more comfortable—yoga pants and her oversized Cavaliers T-shirt—and go around the corner to Tess's place. Tess and Mark, who'd met on a dating app after each of them had gone out with a long string of duds, would be sympathetic to her plight. She could even bring over a bottle of—

"Hey, back off!"

Grant had bared his teeth in a snarl, eyes blazing in the rearview. For a moment, Maggie thought he was snapping at her. Then she realized the headlights behind them were even brighter than before.

"What's he doing?" she asked.

"I don't know. Guy's just got ants in his pants. I'm already ten miles over the speed limit."

Glancing at the dashboard, Maggie saw the needle edge from thirty-five to forty. She grabbed the armrest as the road ahead began to curve. Behind them, she heard the rumble of the other car's engine, its headlights cutting through the back window into her face.

She shifted her position and looked up at Grant, who gripped the wheel tightly. His face wasn't as symmetrical and lean as Dylan's, but he had kind eyes, eyes that suggested he'd seen and done a few things. Maybe even some he wished he could take back.

"Hold on, okay? I think this guy might—"

Before he could finish, Maggie heard a loud crunch of metal and plastic. She was jolted forward, almost smacking her head against the seatback.

"Son of a—!" Grant leaned in over the steering wheel, the car starting to shake.

Maggie looked back at the other car, almost shaking herself. "What're you going to do?"

"Get us the hell out of here."

The engine whined, her body lurching backward. Whirling, she looked for the other car, but it was gone. But where? How had they outrun him so fast? Then she heard the shriek of metal and saw that the other car had crossed the double yellow line and was nosing ahead of them but not passing. Instead, the vehicle cut in toward their lane a little and then swerved back.

Maggie tried to catch her breath but couldn't. "What's he doing?"

"Trying to run us off the road. Don't worry, I won't let him."

Even as Grant said this, the other car swung back in, harder than before. Maggie screamed, her voice drowning out the bleating saxophone from the speakers. A moment later, her whole body was falling to the right, the car's wheels skidding off the road. She closed her eyes, panic squeezing her insides.

Next thing she knew, there was a blur of headlights and flailing branches, and the big round moon turned upside down. It was like being on some awful ride, the kind that spun and rolled too fast, and her cheek smacked something hard, maybe the window, as the seatbelt cut against her chest, and she fell back then lurched forward, her screams turning to sobs, her breath coming in gasps until—

Wham!

Her head swung forward and, when she lifted it again, she saw blood on the spiderwebbed window. At least she was alive. And the crazy ride had stopped. She unclicked her seat belt and leaned into the front. Grant's eyes were shut, a wide streak of blood running from his hairline. When she touched his shoulder, he groaned but didn't say anything.

"You okay?" she asked.

No answer.

She had to get help. She leaned into the door, but it wouldn't budge. She tried and tried again. Finally, she scrambled across the seat to the other door. It shrieked on its hinges but opened. She slid out, holding onto the roof of the car, her legs wobbly.

As she started to come around to the driver's side, she saw something at the top of the embankment. A figure backlit by moonlight, moving toward the overturned car. Maggie hesitated: had someone pulled over to help? Or was this the driver of the other car?

She froze.

Above her, the figure moved closer, feet crunching on dry grass. The silhouette was clearly a woman's. She half-walked, half-slid down the hill, using her right hand to steady herself, holding something in her other hand.

Details came into focus as the figure drew closer. Long dark hair, a thin face, high cheekbones. The woman she'd seen in the bathroom earlier.

But how? And *why*?

The woman stopped about ten feet behind the wrecked car, her face glowing red from the taillights. The object in her left hand was clear now: a long blade with lots of saw-edged teeth, the handle dark black. "You should've stayed away from him," she spat. "I told him that, you know. I said whoever he was going out with, she'd pay the price."

Maggie felt a chill along her back. This must be Dylan's ex. Unbelievable. What was her name, again? Annie? Allison? No, Amanda.

"Listen, Amanda, I barely even know Dylan." Maggie tried to keep her voice steady. "We had a drink, that's it—we didn't even finish before he ran off. He made it perfectly clear he didn't ever want to see me again."

Amanda moved in, holding up the knife. "That's good, because he won't."

"Listen, I—I don't want him. He's yours."

"He sure is." The glint of anger in Amanda's eyes was as sharp as the edge of her knife. "Mine forever."

Maggie felt sick. This was why Dylan had been late for their date. Not because he'd been helping a friend, but because he was dealing with crazy Amanda. That also explained why he'd been all fidgety and run out of the bar in the middle of their date. Because he was afraid she might've followed him. Turned out he was right.

"Seriously, you don't need to worry about me." Maggie glanced at the knife, her throat tightening. "I'm not the competition. He's yours, okay?"

A low moan rose from Amanda's throat. "No!"

"Yes, he is. I swear!"

"He…he doesn't want me anymore."

Maggie didn't know what to say. She felt a twinge of sympathy. She knew all too well what it was like to get dumped by a guy you really cared about, and she could see how it might drive someone over the edge. Maybe not *this* far over. "I'm sorry you broke up, but, uh, you deserve better than him, Amanda. Look at you—you're beautiful. You could have any man you want."

She found it easy to speak with conviction because it was true. Amanda *was* beautiful, and she must've known it.

For a moment, her resolve seemed to flicker, but she kept the blade between them. Maggie brought up her arms by instinct, but there wasn't a lot she could do against that knife, not if Amanda really meant to use it. And Maggie had a feeling she did.

"Dylan's the one I want. The only one I want." Amanda took a step closer, leading with the weapon. "And the only thing in my way is you."

Maggie ran.

She pumped her legs furiously, scanning the darkness ahead, searching for a gap in the wall of brush. Finding a small break, she punched through, feet kicking up dirt and pebbles, breath searing her chest. Amanda came after her, making up ground with her long legs, but Maggie had a good head start, and she might've gotten away.

Except for the log.

It lay in her path like a tired mutt, and by the time she saw it her foot was already coming down on it. The landing was bad enough, throwing her off balance, but then there was a branch hanging down that knocked her back on her butt. She scrambled to her knees and looked up. Amanda was there, face glowing in the moonlight.

She brought the knife down in a flash.

The blade slashed Maggie's thigh, drawing a line of white-hot pain. She howled, squinching her eyes shut, and when she opened them Amanda had the knife up again, eyes glinting with delight. Maggie felt her nerves shriek, blood spilling down her leg, and heard something skittering in the woods behind them. Probably a deer.

Do something. Fast.

She looked over and saw a stone about the size of her closed fist at the base of a nearby tree. If she could grab it, maybe she could even up this fight. Maybe.

"Don't hurt me." Her throat was so tight she could barely get the words out. "Please."

"This is all your fault."

"But I didn't—I'm not—"

"Shut up. If you say one more word, I'll—"

Before Amanda could finish, Maggie's fingers closed around the stone. She hurled it, watched it smash into the side of Amanda's face. Amanda screamed, stumbling back. Maggie tried to get to her feet, but the nerves in her leg shrieked and she lost her footing. Fell.

Amanda moved in again, wearing a mask of pure hatred, a line of blood running down her left cheek. She held the knife low, just above her thigh, her thumb moving back and forth across the blade's flat edge. Faintly, Maggie heard that rustling again.

"You man-stealing slut. You're gonna be sorry."

Amanda was coiled like a snake, ready to strike, but just as she was about to make her move, a shadow crashed out of the brush. At first, Maggie thought the lumbering figure was a bear, then realized it was Grant, her ride-share driver. He knocked Amanda back so hard the knife flew out of her hand.

Maggie dragged herself toward it, felt its sticky grip against her palm. Turning back, she saw that Grant had pinned Amanda. She was writhing beneath him, trying to squirm away.

"Let! Me! Go!"

Grunting and growling, Amanda almost squirted out from beneath Grant's bulky frame, but he grabbed her by the arm and twisted. Maggie realized then that his baggy sweatshirt hid more than just a beer belly. Veins bulged in his throat, his biceps curving as he bent Amanda's arm like a chicken wing.

"How are you?" Grant asked, with a quick glance at Maggie.

"Okay. I just—I thought you were knocked out."

"I was, I guess." Grant touched the dried blood on his scalp. "Your leg doesn't look too good."

Maggie reached for a tree, wincing as she pulled herself upright. "It'll be okay."

On the ground, Amanda squirmed, still trying to get out of Grant's grip. "You're hurting me!"

"Relax, lady." Grant shook his head, smiling at Maggie, showing that gap between his front teeth again. Despite the circumstances, she couldn't help but notice it was cute. "Cops'll be here soon enough."

About a minute later, Maggie heard the wail of sirens, and blue lights strobed across the dark woods. A pair of uniformed police officers loped down the side of the embankment, guns drawn.

"Police! Nobody move!"

The first two officers were followed quickly by two more. They hauled Amanda to her feet and bound her wrists with a pair of plastic cuffs. Another siren wailed, this one an ambulance. Maggie looked down at the gash in her thigh, the first waves of nausea starting to roll through her. Grant put a hand out to make sure she didn't fall.

"You sure you're okay?"

"Yeah. Just a little...."

She couldn't finish, felt herself drift to the ground like a feather. When she looked up, the last thing she saw before blacking out was Grant. He must've caught her as she fell, and all she could see was his face, the gap in his teeth, those kind eyes.

"Thank you," she said, or thought she did. All she really heard was the sound of her own heartbeat as specks of darkness moved in and blotted out the night.

Maggie spent a couple of nights in the hospital, then began physical therapy for her leg. Two weeks after the attack, coming home from one of her more painful sessions, she got a call from Grant. He said he was just checking in. She told him she was doing better, and they chatted for about fifteen minutes. A week later, he called again, and when he called the third time he asked if she wanted to get coffee. He picked her up in his new SUV. The Nissan Sentra had been totaled.

Three months after that, they moved in together. That summer, almost a year to the day after that awful night, Maggie and Grant were married at the Eastwood Farm and Winery, about half a mile from where they'd been run off the road. Tess was the maid of honor, and Grant's brother was the best man. Maggie had to take a break from dancing every couple of songs, but she made it through the night without much pain.

After she and Grant got back from a honeymoon in Paris, they moved into a townhouse in Crozet. Whenever one of their new neighbors heard they were newlyweds and asked how they'd met—as they invariably did—she'd always start with, "It's kind of a long story. I guess you could say it was the ultimate bad date rescue."

Key to the Past

By Cindy Martin

Today marks one hundred and two days.

One hundred and two days since I last slept—really *slept*, meaning more than an hour or two.

The pediatrician tells me to be patient and that Noah will outgrow this brief phase of colic. Clearly, she hasn't experienced manic crying for hours at a time with a red-faced baby. I go through the list of treatments all day: rocking, swaddling, singing, and cranking the volume of static output from a white-noise machine.

My husband has done his best, but five days a week Brad escapes the chaos. I'm not saying my husband's job as a cardiologist at Saint Mary's is easy. He saves lives at one of the most respected hospitals in central Virginia, while I drag myself from room to room in our two-story townhouse, managing laundry, diaper changes, and nursing.

This morning, Brad leans over the bed and gives me a gentle hug.

"I hope the lion is good today," he says.

He uses the nickname I've given our roaring infant. As I return the hug, I inhale his musky cologne and ocean-spray soap and ponder whether I have the energy to shower.

What I'd give to head over to Ironclad Coffee Roasters for a fresh cup, complete with the iconic leaf stencil in my cappuccino. But breastfeeding rules, coupled with a colicky infant, don't recommend caffeine, chocolate, or wine. A trifecta of punishment.

With his loafers in his hands, Brad leaves our bedroom. I roll toward the baby monitor on my nightstand. With the camera pointed downward into Noah's crib, the blueish video glows with the grainy image of my son's little body swaddled in a blanket. Brad's hand appears on the crib railing and then disappears.

The fifth step leading downstairs creaks. Moments later, the front door clicks shut. I glance at the monitor again, relieved that the baby lion is still in la-la-land. The digital clock on my night table reads five-fifteen. I make a mental note to ask Brad why he's been leaving for work half an hour earlier lately.

I embrace the pre-dawn silence, listening to the rhythmic pitter-patter of raindrops. After another restless night, I feel my spine melting into the soft mattress. My eyelids become heavy, and my head sinks into the pillow. A boom of thunder jolts me awake, and I swallow a groan. I'll be stuck indoors all day with a screaming baby. Rain beats on the roof. A gnarly branch of the maple tree scrapes the bedroom window.

On the clock, the red numbers read 7:23. I spring up, shocked that I zonked out for two hours without a peep from Noah. I angle my head toward the baby's room but hear only the steady drumbeat of rain. An icy chill runs through my veins. My mommy-gut flips into action. Grabbing the baby monitor, I stare at the rectangular screen. The fuzzy video displays the changing table—across the room from the crib. I scramble out of bed, my bare feet slapping the floor.

"Noah!" I call out.

My palm smashes the light switch on the nursery wall, illuminating a bedroom big enough for a crib, changing table, dresser, and rocking chair. The crib is empty.

"Noah," I say, my heart hammering. I whirl in a circle, breathless, trying to think. He was here two hours ago—in his crib. The pale yellow walls blur. I stumble toward my bedroom, where I rip my phone from its charger and punch in Brad's number.

"Pick up, Brad," I mumble, dashing toward the end of the hallway and into the home office that doubles as a guest room.

Voicemail. I shout into the phone, "Come on, Brad. Where the hell are you?"

I call again and again.

Racing back into Noah's room, I make sure I'm not losing my mind. Lack of sleep has caused me to see and hear things that aren't there, like the pale face of Amanda, my long-missing half-sister. Why her, of all people?

I check the crib again, but Noah still isn't there. With shaking fingers, I hit 911.

"Henrico County Police, what's your emerg—"

"My baby is missing," I scream. "Noah Halmon. Help me!"

The dispatcher tells me to calm down, then asks for my name, address, and a description of Noah.

"My name is Heather Halmon. Noah's mom. He's a hundred and two days old. I mean a little over three months. Thirteen pounds, twenty-four inches. Blue eyes and brown hair. He can't even roll over in his crib, let alone run off. You have to find him."

"Officers are on the way," the dispatcher says.

Tears stream down my cheeks. The dispatcher tells me to stay on the line, and I see Brad's face light up on my screen. I tap over to his call, taking the stairs two at a time.

"Is Noah with you?" My words border on hysterical.

"What? No. Heather, what's going on?"

"He's not in his crib. The police are coming." I'm half-sobbing. Over the pounding rain, I hear the clank of dishware. "Where are you?"

"Hospital cafeteria. I'm leaving now."

I switch back to the dispatcher, who tells me officers are less than two minutes away. I turn on all the lights downstairs. It doesn't matter that I know Noah couldn't have gotten out of his crib on his own. I race through the den, half bath, laundry area, and dining room, searching. The kitchen, which overlooks the parking lot, is empty, too. No sign of my baby boy anywhere. I open the front door and run down the wooden steps. Within seconds, my white UVA T-shirt is plastered to my skin.

"Noah!" I scream his name, my head swinging from one direction to the other.

Neighbors on both sides of my unit are preparing for their day. Kids are loaded into cars, and briefcases swing from one arm while gym mats are tucked under the other. The man from next door gets out of his car and hurries to my side. Steady rain pelts us both.

I practically run at him. "Noah's missing!"

"Did you call the police?"

"Yes." I lift my phone. The dispatcher is still on the line.

Other residents witnessing my distress come to my side. Faces shift in and out of focus. The pavement sways. Black specks swirl in my eyes. I tilt my head back and feel a gentle hand moving me toward my covered porch.

Two police cars turn into the parking lot, lights glowing. Sending the neighbors home, the uniformed cops instruct me to stay put while they search my home.

A stocky man in a khaki trench coat holding a black umbrella approaches.

"I'm Detective Jeremy Bey, Henrico County Police." He opens his coat, revealing a badge on his hip. "You are Mrs. Heather Halmon, correct?"

I nod.

"I'll be right with you. Let me confirm the house is secure," Detective Bey says.

My next-door neighbor returns to his car and turns off the ignition. He hunches his shoulders, dashes toward his front door, and enters his darkened home. Others do the same. I can't help wondering if evil lurks behind one of those doors.

Detective Bey waves me inside and hands me a towel he picked up off the pile of unfolded laundry.

"You need to find Noah," I say, hearing the pleading in my voice. "My baby is gone."

"We're searching." Detective Bey rubs the crown of his smooth, tanned head and escorts me into the kitchen, pulling a chair from the oval table.

My skin prickles. A memory comes flooding back. Cops sitting at my childhood kitchen table in Charlottesville with my parents after Amanda disappeared. I was only six, listening from my bedroom door. Those cops searched, too, but they never found her. This, right now, feels surreal, and I collapse on the chair.

"How could a baby just vanish from a crib?"

"That's what I'm here to find out." Detective Bey removes his coat, draping it on the back of the chair. He pulls out a pen and notepad from his pocket and takes a seat across from me. "Walk me through your morning, please."

I squeeze my palms together in my lap to stop the trembling, panic seizing my heart. My imagination goes wild with all kinds of horrific scenarios.

"Take your time," he says.

I nod and release the breath I didn't realize I was holding. "We're talking about a two-hour gap." I run through the timeline and tell him both doors and all windows were locked.

It hits me then. The baby cam records video for twenty-four hours. I open up the app on my cell and rewind the footage to where Brad's hand leaves the crib rail. I hit play. The murky video shows Noah lying still until the timestamp of 5:51 AM.

I share my screen with the detective. "Look!"

The camera angle doesn't show anyone coming close to the crib, but suddenly the lens spins a hundred and eighty degrees from the crib to the wall, settling on the changing table. I crank the volume. A slight rustling sound.

"I need to ask you this," the detective says, his words slow. "I know you're an exhausted mother. Any chance you got up and put Noah somewhere, and then forgot where?"

"Are you serious? You think I took my baby out of his crib and hid him like some psycho mom? And turned the camera, too?"

"Look, Mrs. Halmon, we've had situations with insomniacs, sleepwalkers, and other issues."

I rake my fingers through my unwashed hair and sob. Swiping my tears with the heel of my hand, I stare out the window. Officers knock on doors, search vehicles, and comb through bushes. Brad's Tesla splashes through the pond-like parking lot littered with patrol cars. I race outside, falling into his arms.

"Noah is gone," I moan into his shoulder.

He guides me into the house and toward the kitchen. Detective Bey introduces himself.

"Any news?" Brad asks the other man.

I notice Brad is wearing khakis and a polo, not his usual dark slacks and dress shirt, but it doesn't matter right now.

"Our department is issuing a BOLO—a Be On the Look Out report. Can you text me the latest photo of your son?" Detective Bey places his business card with his phone number on the table.

I scroll through the photos app and send him a picture of Noah with a gummy smile from two days ago. The picture makes me cry again. Through the madness of my days and nights, I'd almost forgotten how lovely my boy is.

"I've reached out to the FBI for their assistance," Detective Bey says. "I'll be working with their CARD unit, which is the Child Abduction Rapid Deployment team."

"What about an AMBER Alert?" I look up from Noah's photo on my phone.

"The FBI will make that determination. Stranger abductions are extremely rare."

I spread my arms. "As you can see, Brad doesn't have Noah, and neither do I." Fresh tears well.

"I know you're frustrated, but we're moving as fast as we can," the detective says.

Crime-show and mystery-novel plots about missing-child cases flash through my head. The parents are always the first suspects. That's exactly what happened in my half-sister's case, twenty years ago. Amanda argued with my father, saying he loved me more than her. My dad tried to reason with her. Amanda slammed the door and left.

My father told my mom, "Let her blow off some steam. She'll show up at her mother's house."

She didn't. The next day, my dad called the police, but since Amanda was seventeen years old—almost an adult—it took about a week for law enforcement to investigate her disappearance. By the time the detectives grilled my parents and cleared them, my half-sister was long gone. Her oval face, framed with straight black hair and dark makeup circling her piercing blue eyes, is etched into my memory.

Today, Amanda would be almost forty years old. I've often wondered if she's alive. My father spent years trying to find her and following up with the Charlottesville Police. After he passed, my mother and I didn't keep up the search, assuming we were the last two people on earth Amanda would want to see. But it gnawed at me. How could someone vanish like that?

Now Noah is missing. He certainly didn't leave on his own, but the sense of helplessness is the same.

Two women dressed in identical navy-blue jackets embossed with the Henrico County Police logo enter. They nod at us and climb the stairs. On their backs are the bold white letters CSI. A huge white truck with royal blue lettering that reads *FBI Mobile Command Center* pulls into the parking lot.

Detective Bey opens the front door to a petite and slender woman in a taupe suit. She has a flawless bronze complexion and a short Afro. Behind her, a man with cropped brown hair and black-rimmed glasses tilts his head down a few inches to avoid hitting the doorframe.

"I'm Special Agent Kiara Eddy with the FBI, here in Richmond. This is my partner, Special Agent Joseph Lewis."

Brad and I shake their hands.

"I'm Brad Halmon, and this is my wife Heather."

"We'll be assisting Henrico County in finding your son. As you probably know, the first few hours after a child has gone missing are critical," Special Agent Eddy says. "We want to start right away by interviewing both of you. Separately."

"Why?" I ask. "We've got nothing to hide from each other or you." I look at Brad and back at the agents.

"It's protocol," she says in response. They remove their rain gear, and I hang their jackets on the coat rack in the entryway.

Special Agent Lewis escorts Brad into the den. The female agent suggests I change into something dry. She follows me up the stairs and remains outside my bedroom door. I toss my wet clothes into the hamper and pick up my Chincoteague Island sweatshirt from a long-ago vacation. I pull it over my head and yank on leggings and socks.

Glancing at the forensic team in my baby's room, I flinch and swallow hard. Special Agent Eddy guides me back to the kitchen table.

Detective Bey tells her that the K-9s have arrived, and he heads out into the storm.

Special Agent Eddy picks up a cup from the clean dishrack, fills it with water from the fridge, and places it in front of me. I glance at the microwave clock. 10:17. It feels as if days have passed, rather than a few hours.

"You didn't hear anything after your husband left?" Special Agent Eddy asks.

"Like I told the detective, it's unusual for me to sleep in or sleep at all. Typically, Noah is up around six, and I am, too. If he cried, I would have heard him."

"Okay. Who has access to your house? Family, friends, any services?"

"My handyman, cleaning lady, and my sister-in-law have keys. I can't imagine any of them kidnapping Noah."

"I'll need their contact info."

"Are you suggesting someone we know took Noah?" My stomach flutters.

"We won't know until we investigate."

I scroll the contacts in my phone and read off the names and numbers. The agent taps the information into an email.

Could it be someone we know? All of this has me thinking about how well I know the people who come in and out of my house. I mentally run through the list. Brad's sister Mary, but I'm sure she's fine. We're family. Teresa has been cleaning my house for a couple of years, and on several occasions she's even offered to babysit. I think that might have been Brad's idea, but I don't have the energy to go on a date. Then there's handyman Sam. He has a heart of gold, even went above and beyond helping me kidproof the townhouse. No way he would hurt my son.

Special Agent Lewis appears in the archway. Brad is standing behind him, staring at the floor, his arms hanging by his side. "I'm taking Brad to the office," Lewis says.

"What? No." I jump to my feet. "What's going on?" I rush toward Brad, but the towering agent steps between us.

"Heather, your husband will be taking a polygraph test," Special Agent Lewis says.

"Why?"

"We have some concerns. I'll explain later." He directs Brad toward the door.

"Brad," I scream after him. "What have you done?"

I watch them leave from the kitchen window. TV news vans litter the parking lot. A gaggle of cameramen are gathered behind the crime-scene tape, recording this moment.

I look into Special Agent Eddy's wide, earthy eyes. "Did Brad do something to our baby?"

"Special Agent Lewis is doing his job, Mrs. Halmon, that's all." She sits with perfect posture and crosses her arms on her chest. "How is your marriage?"

"Okay, I guess. Between the baby and his job as a doctor, we are two ships in the night." I pause. "Is Brad having an affair?"

"Again, we're crossing our t's and dotting our i's," Special Agent Eddy says.

I touch my aching right breast, feeling the dampness through my sweatshirt—a painful reminder I haven't fed Noah today.

She reads the signals well. "Heather, let's take a break."

I head upstairs, escaping to my bedroom. After starting the breast pump, I feel physical relief, but my heart and head throb. I cry softly, thinking about Noah—and Brad.

I hear a male voice downstairs. Detective Bey, with his Boston accent, is back. The fifth stair creaks. I look at the monitor. The camera has been uprighted and points at the door of the nursery with the police tape. Images of Special Agent Eddy and Detective Bey fill the small screen. I turn off the pump when I hear the detective's voice coming through the baby cam.

"There's no sign of breaking and entering," says Detective Bey. "Our K-9 found a key under the front porch. I assume it fell through the cracks.

Literally."

Special Agent Eddy nods. "It fits the front door?"

I remember the key I lost a few weeks ago.

"Yes. On the keyring is a plastic tag to the Ironclad Coffee Roasters café. I had them run the QR code, one of those frequent-flier memberships where if you buy fifteen coffees in a month, you get a free one. The code is linked to an account for an Amy Maxwell."

Who the hell is Amy Maxwell?

"And the punch line?" the female agent asks.

"As of a few weeks ago, Amy and Brad have been meeting for coffee. Five-thirty every morning, before work." Detective Bey holds up his index finger. "But *this* morning, the barista says the hubby sat there for an hour and a half, alone, with two lattes on a table. Then he left in a hurry."

My chin trembles. I want to scream. *My husband has been cheating on me.*

"It'll be interesting to see the results of the polygraph," Special Agent Eddy says.

"And my guys tracked down the maid service lady. She's clean."

"Dear Lord, stop the puns, please."

"But Sam the handyman could be up to something. We found a boatload of baby food and disposable bibs at his place. He claims they're for his elderly mother." Detective Bey swipes at his egg-like head. "Sam also told us that, two weeks ago, Heather called him to say she'd lost her housekey while out with Noah. It's odd she called the handyman and not her husband. Sam said he got a new key made the same day."

"What are you thinking?' the female agent asks.

"Doubtful there's a fling happening between Sam and Heather. Honestly, I'm more worried she had enough of the crying kid and…you know. I don't want to say Susan Smith or Andrea Yates."

My chest is so tight, it feels like it might explode. *How dare he say that?*

"I'm not getting that vibe," Special Agent Eddy says. "Let's keep a team on Sam. Where does Amy Maxwell live?"

"Right here. Across the parking lot."

"No," I say, clamping my hands over my mouth.

The cops move out of frame and knock on my door.

"Coming," I say. I change out of my damp sweatshirt into something dryer and pull open the door.

"How much did you hear?" Special Agent Eddy asks.

"All of it."

A long minute passes.

"I'm sorry," Detective Bey says finally.

I'm having none of that. Anger spews from my mouth. "So the headlines are my husband and I are cheating on one another, and I might have killed Noah?"

"Heather, Mrs. Halmon, we apologize for our unprofessionalism," Special Agent Eddy says.

I wave a hand at them. I don't care what they think of me, I just want Noah back.

"Who is Amy Maxwell? If she lives across the parking lot, I bet she's the nurse I ran into when I had Noah in the stroller." I point out the bedroom window. "Over there. Wilde Lake. She's middle-aged, short blond hair, wears scrubs. She told me she was a home healthcare nurse." The words spill from my mouth as fast as I think them. "I bet she stole my key from the stroller cupholder." Adrenaline surges through every part of me. "Let's go find her."

Detective Bey lifts a palm. "We're already doing that, Mrs. Halmon. You need to let us handle this."

I push past him, racing down the stairs, the investigators on my heels. An officer stands at the door, blocking my exit. I rush to the kitchen window, raising the blinds. More officers are herding the media toward Wilde Lake Drive—the entrance of the development—and away from our house.

"We have intelligence that indicates she's home." Detective Bey shrugs into his raincoat and opens the door. "That's all I can say right now."

A moment later, Brad steps through the door, dark half-moon circles under his eyes. Special Agent Lewis follows him inside. "Brad passed the polygraph test."

My husband comes toward me, reaching out, but I step back.

"I'm sorry for being a shitty husband and father," he says. "Nothing happened. Honest."

"I don't want to hear it," I say through clenched teeth. "This is all your fault. Seeing a nurse when—" I can't finish the sentence.

The sound of helicopters rumbling overhead sends me back to the window, and I press my face to the glass. Reporters, getting as close as they can, scramble to get the best live shots. More FBI vans swing into the lot. My stomach flip-flops as I watch the scene outside unfold.

Police officers and FBI agents in dark tactical clothing and vests climb out of vans with guns drawn. They spread out around Amy's house, taking strategic positions in every direction.

A deep male voice shouts, "FBI!" The team waits. My heart thunders in my chest. They call out again. When there's no response, they break the door down. Minutes later, the team emerges with one officer holding a clear evidence bag holding a cell phone.

"A decoy," Special Agent Eddy says behind me.

The officers pile into the Command Center truck. Seconds later, the vans are gone. Amy is gone. Hope drains from my soul.

Detective Bey bolts into the house. He huddles with Eddy and Lewis in the den. My cell blares with the familiar AMBER Alert tone. This time it's my son featured, along with Amy and a navy-blue sedan. I slump onto a kitchen chair, too spent to move. Brad sits across from me.

"I'm sorry. I can't believe I didn't see through Amy's story," my husband says.

I don't look at him.

"She targeted me. No doubt. She said she had a son with a heart defect and asked for advice. She said she's a single mother and doesn't have time for friends. She happened to be in the hospital's cafeteria during my lunch many days. I felt like she really needed help, so we exchanged phone numbers. She told me she lived in Short Pump but closer to Town Center. She wanted to meet up at Ironclad. One meeting turned into a few. I figured I could help her son. It felt good to be needed."

My head shoots up. "And you're not needed *here*?"

"I'm an idiot." Brad attempts to touch my hand, but I pull away. "She begged me to meet her this morning and help her through something, so I called in sick. I don't know what I was thinking."

I glance at our wedding photo on the wall, at our smiling faces. We were such different people three years ago. Both of us.

"I think Amy targeted me, too. She must have been watching us," I say at last. I believe it. What I don't understand is why.

Hours pass. The sky boasts streaks of gold and pink. Like a scene from the old Hitchcock movie, *Rear Window*, Brad and I watch our neighbors return home with their kids from soccer, gymnastics, and the grocery. My heart aches at the sight of everyday life, of normalcy.

Special Agent Lewis's phone buzzes, and he walks into the den. I follow his every move. When he returns, a grin fills his face.

"We found Noah. He's safe and on his way home."

I stand on wobbly legs, and Brad wraps me in a hug. "Where is he?" I say.

"Florida. A State Trooper got the AMBER Alert and spotted a blue sedan with Virginia plates at a rest area. Noah was in a car seat in Amy's vehicle. He was strapped in and pretty angry."

Our little lion. I laugh so hard, the tears flow again.

"Can we go get him?" Brad asks.

"We need you to stay here. Amy is in custody, and we have a medic examining Noah. He'll be here in about four hours."

Detective Bey joins us. "Heather, there's someone here with a gift for you."

Sam follows the detective into the kitchen, carrying a case of little jars. "I never thought buying bulk baby food at Costco could lead to a police investigation," he says, setting the flat on the kitchen counter. "I got a good deal and thought I'd split it between you and my mother."

I laugh again and hug him. "I'm so sorry you got caught up in this."

"No worries." Sam nods to all of us and leaves.

I'd never doubted him, but I have another question for Special Agent Lewis. Facing him, I ask, "How did the key Amy stole get under our porch?"

"We're interviewing Amy now, but we assume it fell from her hand or pocket while she was leaving your house and slipped through the planks."

"I still can't believe she set Brad up in that café, then waltzed in here and stole our baby. And why?"

No one has an answer.

Hours later, headlights flash in the parking lot. The agents and Detective Bey escort us outside. Despite the early morning hour, the street and lot are alive with neighbors and camera crews lining the path from our front step to the SUV.

Special Agent Eddy reaches into the rear seat, unstraps Noah, and hands him to me. Together, Brad and I smother him in kisses. After the media people get their video of a happy reunion, we return home. I hold Noah like I'll never let him go.

"What happened?" Brad asks. "Did you find out why Amy took Noah?"

Special Agent Lewis looks from Brad to me, his gaze piercing. "We confirmed that Amy Maxwell isn't her real name. It's Amanda Riley."

My mouth drops open, but now everything makes sense—sort of. Those times I imagined I saw my half-sister weren't delusions. "Amanda? Wow. She's changed. Taller, thin, and blond. But I still don't understand why she took my boy."

"We don't have the full story, but it's something about how you stole her father, so she wanted to take something from you," Special Agent Lewis says.

"Really? I wasn't even born when my dad and her mom got divorced. I can't believe she held a grudge all these years and then came after our son. That's insane."

"You'd be surprised by the motives of crimes we encounter," Special Agent Eddy says. "At least this one has a happy ending."

"And we solved two cases in one day." Special Agent Lewis says.

"And, hey, there's another silver lining: Noah isn't crying." Detective Bey looks over at me. "Maybe a car ride is the solution."

Brad takes my hand. "Heather, maybe we should try that. We could start with a family trip to Ironclad for a few decafs." He squeezes my hand. "I think we have some things to talk about."

"We certainly do," I say, squeezing back. "We certainly do."

The Golden Girl

By Carol Willis

He crouched in the alley, watching Melva scrounge for leftovers. Smelly old bitch. The midnight air filled with the pong of stale beer and rotting food. A bead of sweat trickled down his neck.

Melva hummed and licked her fingers, digging deeper into the trash. Crazy, as well as disgusting.

Hoots and raucous laughter from Main Street. Closing time.

He ran his thumb over his blade. A serene calm descended, enveloping him like a darkening shade, chilling his heart with an icy wash.

Go time.

He stepped out of the shadows and into the weak light of the alley.

Melva lifted her head and turned. "Who's there?"

He strode toward her. He would show her who. He'd show them all.

Melva squinted through the dim. A cat mewed at her feet.

He sidled up to her and waited. A time too fleeting, really. Short as the span between heartbeats when fear and confusion turn to recognition. But never respect. That was the thing.

"Oh," she said, leaning away from him, clutching a greasy waxed wrapper. Her hands trembled with the shakes. She licked her lips. "I recognize you," she said, her tone mocking now.

How dare she.

"I recognize you, too," he said, smiling.

Then he did what he had come to do.

Ginny leaned against the doorjamb opposite Terry's Bar and waited.

Kicked out. Again.

The Cavaliers sign in the front window blinked, a chaotic, dizzying technicolor of neon oranges and blues. The last customer exited, wassailing as he staggered away. Bernie, the waitress, sat at the bar alone. Ginny wanted to apologize for spilling beer and not leaving a tip.

Bernie. Bernadine "Sanitary" Namkin, from the low-rent housing development off Jefferson Street. Pudgy and slow, everyone had teased her. Middle school, a cruel and unforgiving place for people like Bernie. Except Bernie wasn't pudgy anymore. Not beautiful, but sexy and plentiful in all the right places.

Ginny regretted her actions, more for having made fun of Bernie growing up than for cheating her out of a tip. She had spent the last of her money on the beer, so she couldn't have tipped, anyway.

God, she was such a jerk.

Her body ached for another pint. Or better yet, a whiskey.

She swallowed. It was too late to get money anywhere else. She fingered the chain around her neck, the gold and jade Capricorn pendant smooth and warm to the touch, and thought of Sonny's Pawn Shop on Main. But Sonny was a cheap son of a bitch and wouldn't give her much for it. It wasn't even her necklace. Earlier today, she had stolen it from Leilani, her roommate, high as fuck and passed out on the couch.

Ginny skittered around the corner and headed down the alley behind Terry's. "Fuck y'all!" she whooped.

"Shut up, crazy bitch!" someone yelled, but she could not tell where it was coming from.

Halfway down the alley, Smelva was on the ground, legs splayed, leaning against the dumpster. Her name was Melva, but everyone always called her Smelva because she smelled like boiled cabbage, always hanging out behind the bar, begging for a drink. Melva had worked in the middle school cafeteria and had stunk even then. Mean to almost everyone but Ginny, saving the purple Pixy Stix and sneaking them to her once a week.

A mangy cat slinked out of the shadows and licked at a sticky puddle next to Smelva.

Ginny could smell the reek from twenty feet away. The cat meowed.

Still, under the influence of weak beer and leftover guilt, she felt for the necklace again. What the heck. She undid the clasp. Money from the necklace would tide Smelva over for a day or two.

She held out the gold chain. The pendant gleamed, catching the light of the weak sodium streetlamp. "Here. It's all I got."

Instead of reaching up and taking the necklace, Smelva sat there, unmoving. The pendant swayed hypnotically.

"Hey, Melva," Ginny said, and waggled the necklace in front of the old woman's face. "I said, do you want this?"

She jostled Smelva's bare foot, and the body careened to the right, head landing on the pavement with a sickening thud. It was only then Ginny noticed a dark splotch on her neck, like an oil slick oozing down her front.

"What the hell, Smelv?" But she already knew the answer. A jagged cut on the side of the old woman's neck gaped open. On the ground next to her, what Ginny had taken for a puddle of water was blood, already viscous and congealing, its metallic odor mingling with the smell of boiled cabbage and rotting food. She kicked the cat, who mewled in protest.

Ginny recoiled, stumbling backward. She considered going back to Terry's, but Smelva was dead. No use calling an ambulance. The EMTs might think she had something to do with it. The last thing she needed was the police riding her ass.

She stuffed the necklace inside her bra and scarpered down the alley, glancing behind her as she dodged potholes and piles of trash.

Bernadine swirled the straw in her Tom Collins, her limbs already melty. Highball number three on top of the vodka tonics she'd been knocking back all shift. It was her favorite time of day. After closing time, nursing as many drinks as Terry would allow. He always played older rock music, like Tom Petty and Stevie Nicks. Not the grunge and hip-hop the university kids liked.

Terry walked in from the alley and wiped his hands on a bar towel. "What's up, Bern?" he asked, gathering lemons and limes next to the sink.

She shrugged. "Nada."

"Saw you take one down the front," he said, sharpening a fruit knife. "That girl is a regular—a regular skanky-ass bitch."

Bernadine snorted. "Yep."

It was going to take more than vodka and gin to make the ache in her chest go away. This wasn't the first time a customer had spilled a drink on her. But the fact it had been *her*. Gigi, of all people. It was just like her to sit at a table, obliging Bernadine to wait on her. Bring her drinks. Then, when she spilled beer down Bernadine's blouse, act like it was *her* fault. And didn't leave a tip. It was middle school all over again.

Gigi. Ginny Golden—the fucking Golden Girl. Teacher's pet, Homecoming Queen, every guy's wet dream.

Tom Petty was singing about his heart being dragged around. Bernadine knew how he felt. She sucked the last of her drink and slid off the barstool.

"Night, Terry."

"Night, B." Terry reached into his pocket for the keys. "You should go out the front."

"Nah. Don't bother. I'll go out the back," Bernadine said, concentrating on enunciating each word.

The metal door closed behind her with a heavy *thunk*, plunging her into the deep shadow of the building. Down the alley, Smelva was passed out in front of the dumpster. A cat meowed from a darkened alcove.

Bernadine walked in the opposite direction.

She was usually skittish, but tonight—maybe because she was already drunk, or maybe because her feet ached, or because the night was warm and humid—she felt sluggish. Her thoughts drifted, and she struggled to stay alert.

The night sky was cloudy, and a gust of warm air scattered trash along the pavement. An old sign scraped on rusty hinges. The bars closed early on a weeknight, and Water Street was deserted. She caught the faint whiff of a burned match as footsteps approached from behind, but when she turned around, no one was there.

Ginny emerged from the alley and turned onto Water Street. Bernie was up ahead, weaving her way toward the Downtown Mall. Still unsettled from finding Smelva's body, Ginny wasn't ready to face Leilani, so she followed Bernie on impulse. She'd get to apologize, after all.

She slowed her pace, watched Bernie open a weathered door with peeling paint and disappear into a crumbling brick apartment building. She waited. A light switched on behind a window on the second floor.

Gotcha.

She waited five minutes or so to let Bernie get settled, then pushed open the front door. There was no lock. It was not that kind of place. Down the hall, a television blared. As she crept up the rickety staircase to the second floor, ancient wood planks creaked. The air was thick with a flinty odor, like the inside of a tinderbox. Shadows oozed from crevices in the wall.

A sliver of light shone beneath the second door on the right. Z95.1 played on the radio. She tapped on the door. "Bernie?"

Footsteps approached. "Yeah? Who is it?"

"It's Ginny, Bern. Gigi," she said, wincing. She knew Bernie would not be happy to see her. Her buzz was wearing off, and this suddenly seemed like a bad idea. "From Terry's," she added.

There was no answer.

"I'm sorry. I know this is kind of weird. I came to apologize," she said, keeping an eye on the thickening shadows, like shapeshifters in the corner. A floorboard groaned. "I'm sorry about the beer … and everything." She wasn't good at this.

The door creaked open. A thin rectangle of light sliced through the darkness. Bernie was dressed in a white camisole without a bra, hips pouring out of black-lace panties. She held a wineglass in one hand.

"You must be hard up, if you're apologizing to me," Bernie slurred, giving Ginny the once over. "I thought you were some creeper," she said, scanning the darkened hallway.

Ginny glanced behind her. "Nope. Just me. Creeping 'round your back stairs," she said, eliciting a tiny smile from Bernie. "Can I come in a sec? I promise not to spill anything."

With glazed eyes, Bernie appeared to consider.

"I swear." Ginny held up her hands in mock surrender.

"Fine," Bernie said, resigned, her eyelids drooping. She took a sip of wine, and the red liquid sloshed up the sides. She was drunk, or well on her way.

Ginny stepped inside. "Thanks."

"I got wine. And vodka in the freezer." Bernie turned and walked to the fridge, the dimples on her milky thighs winking. Now that Ginny was here, she seemed glad for the company.

Ginny's ears perked up at the sound of vodka. Neat and cold. The perfect ticket to chase her fading buzz. "Vodka would be great. I'm sorry about the beer," she said, babbling. The thought of cold booze made her downright loquacious.

Bernie shrugged, handing her a generous pour. "Okay."

The vodka was cool and slippery in her mouth. It felt good. "Thanks. I know I don't deserve this," she said, lifting the glass and giving Bernie a toast.

"Thought I would save you the trouble of asking," Bernie said. "I know you."

Ginny nodded, unsure if Bernie meant *I know you're an asshole* or *I know you're a drunk*. Both would be correct. She knocked back the vodka and wiped her mouth. "I don't think Terry likes me," she said.

Bernie poured her another. "He knows you're a regular."

Ginny sipped, feeling the alcohol working its way through her. By twenty-five, already considered a regular at the seediest bar in town, home to only the most dedicated alcoholics.

Look at me now, ma!

It hadn't always been this way. Growing up, she had lived across town in an upscale neighborhood next to the high school. Outgoing and popular, once upon a time, like the golden-haired princess in a fairy tale. Everyone praised her, gave her things. Like the Pixy Stix. *You've got it all, Golden Girl,* her teachers said, with a wink and a smile, calling her Gigi. *A real shooting star.*

High school. Summer party after junior year. Halter top and brand-new white cutoffs, spritzing J'adore behind her knees. Throngs of rising seniors flocking around trashcan punch like moths to a flame, dancing to a car stereo *whomp-whomp*ing. A rando hands her a red cup. Purple brew goes down sweet and sticky. The ground tilts, the black night pitching. Then falling, tumbling backward, the trees flung upside down.

Guys laughing. Whispers in the dark.

Skanky bitch. Filthy cow.

Flat on her back, she wakes tits up. White cutoffs stained with red dirt and purple vomit. A meteor shower streaking the night sky with its tears, the crickets serrating a dirge.

Roofied. Knocked out and knocked about.

Alcohol and pills. Searching for solace at the bottom of every bottle. An OD. The ER. The stint in Fishersville, that hellhole.

Why did you try to kill yourself, honey?

"You're such a fuckup," her brother said.

From shooting star to setting sun.

Ginny Golden. Nothing but fool's gold all along.

Bernie tugged at a strap, her breasts straining against the cheap polyester fabric. Her nipples were dark round nubs. There was something pornographic about this, so Ginny stared at the smooth pink skin of her neck instead. She thought of Smelva's dead body. The gash on her neck, mouth wide open.

The necklace had become a burden. The pendant dug into Ginny's skin. The singe of stolen goods. She reached into her bra and pulled it out.

Bernie eyed her curiously.

Ginny held it out. "I wanted to give you this. For...being such a jerk."

Bernie took the necklace, her eyes never leaving the gold and jade pendant.

"It was a present from my brother," Ginny lied.

She needed the necklace to be gone. An act of absolution. As if she could negate her theft and vindicate herself from all the times she had been shitty to Bernie and everyone else, including poor dead Smelva.

Bernie seemed pleased but wary. "It's pretty. Looks expensive." She set her wine glass down, holding the necklace up to the light. "Why are you giving it to me?"

"It's not really my thing."

But Bernie was not paying attention, too captivated to care. She clasped the necklace around her neck, her brow furrowed in concentration.

"It suits you," Ginny said.

It was an odd exchange, but Bernie was odd and desperate enough to accept it.

Relieved, Ginny murmured another apology and left. Bernie stayed where she was, drunk and muzzy, the green and gold pendant dangling above the blink of her cleavage.

Main Street heaved with students emptying from the bars, turnt and shit-talking. As Ginny passed through a herd of frat boys on the Corner, she stumbled on a crack in the sidewalk, still unsteady from the vodka. The smell of Christian's Pizza made her stomach roil.

She turned onto Page and hoped none of them followed. Sobriety dragged her insides, the comedown after a good buzz. Bloated and queasy. A headache already knocking.

She passed the boarded-up blue house on the right, not able to shake the feeling of having been followed. The front porch was caved in on one side. Two lawn chairs sat empty in a patch of weeds. A pile of crushed cans formed a lopsided pyramid next to them. She turned right and took off her shoes, her feet rubbed raw from the cheap-ass strappy heels. Up the hill, Westhaven—the ugly beige public housing complex—squatted alongside the railroad.

A lowrider crouched on the street ahead of her. The skirl of music rocked the car as Lizzo rapped. Ginny felt the thumping of the bass. The windows were down, and the cloying smell of weed made her insides lurch.

"I want me some of that," a guy said from the driver's side. "Damn girl, why don't you come over here?" Someone else snickered, invisible in the backseat.

Ginny scooted to the curb on the opposite side of the street.

She turned onto the nearest footpath, a trail of packed dirt, still one building shy of her own, when the deep *thunk* of a car door sounded behind her. The hairs on her arms rose, the base of her spine tingled. She remembered Smelva.

She ran now, her bare feet crunching on broken glass.

Fuck!

She hopped on one foot, aware of someone creeping in the shadows. Footfalls sneaking behind her. A darkness in the dark. Someone shoved her down.

A heaviness descended. Something solid and firm. Like a mattress toppling, pinning her under.

Ginny woke, sweating. It was dark, a dim light came from somewhere far away. The smell of vomit hit her. And something else, like a burned match, lingered beneath the pungent odor.

Sharp pain coalesced behind her eyes, shooting stars at the edges of her vision. She squeezed her eyes shut, and her stomach clenched, heaving until she collapsed onto her side. The sensation of spinning so strong, she thought something was turning her around and around.

"Stop. Please stop," she whimpered.

A susurrus in her ear.

Skank.

Then a bang on a door. "Hey! Who's in there?"

The bawl of a police siren. Blue flashing lights. The spinning stopped. Footsteps running away.

She lay back, grimacing, surrendering to the darkness again.

Her eyelids fluttered. Darkness turned dull gray, like swimming up from the deep. Her head was heavy, the pain now a dull ache.

Someone tapped her shoulder.

Wake up, skank.

She jerked, tugging hard against metal bed rails.

"What?" Her voice came out a croak, her throat dry and scratchy.

"Whoa, we don't want to lose the IV," said a friendly voice near her ear.

Soft restraints encircled her wrists. She opened her eyes to a curtained room, straining to focus. The smell of vomit and burned matches was gone.

"You're awake." A man in rumpled green scrubs peered down at her. His face sagged with fatigue, and a stethoscope snaked around his neck. A deep purple birthmark stretched along his temple and crawled under his hairline. She had the weird impulse to reach up and wipe it off.

"Shh. It's okay. I got you," he said. "I'm the ER resident. Dr. Zhou. Do you remember how you got here?" He reached up and adjusted a clear bag of fluids. A cool rush in the crook of her arm made her think of vodka.

Who had whispered to her? Had it been real?

Ginny closed her eyes, trying to make sense of things. Discomfiting yet familiar. The ER. The tang of antiseptic—the smell she had been trying to place—mingled with the fluorescent lighting, tinkle of metal, and hushed voices behind curtains, like a cocktail party down the hall.

Dr. Zhou. That distinctive birthmark. Middle school—eighth-grade social studies. Ash Zhou. The shy little kid who sat behind Bernie and picked his nose. Everyone called him the boy with the spider tattoo. Even Bernie had taunted him.

A knot pressed on the top of her head, lost along the rough edges of a fractured memory. High school again. The summer party after junior year. He had been there, too, hadn't he?

Hey, boy with the spider tattoo, your turn. Go! Go! Go!

Heckling followed by rowdy jeers.

Smelva's dead body. Blood leeching onto the pavement next to her bare feet.

A sharp pain pricked behind Ginny's eyes.

Dr. Zhou said something, and the pain disappeared. The relief so overwhelming, she wanted to weep.

"See? I told you I got you. Neuro is on their way." He leaned closer. "Can you tell me anything about last night?"

She shook her head, but dizziness overtook her.

Dr. Zhou said, "Don't move your head. Sorry, I should have said that sooner."

"No shit." Her tongue flopped, a pink slug in her mouth.

He moved to the head of her bed. "Don't worry, your memory will come back. It may take a while." He patted her—light touches, like a spider scrabbling across her shoulder.

Ginny shuddered and closed her eyes.

When she opened them again, he was not there.

She felt for the necklace, but it was gone. Terry's bar. The alley. She had given the necklace to Smelva. No, Smelva was dead. She had given it to Bernie. Why had she done that? Bernie's dark nipples straining to be free.

The memory of last night dissolved beyond reach, like a bad dream.

"Someone clocked you good," Leilani said. She stood next to the hospital bed, a white plastic CVS bag twisted around her wrist, reeking of weed and tobacco. "You hear Smelva bought it?" she asked, swiping her finger across her neck, her head bobbing with inappropriate laughter.

"Huh?" Ginny's vision clouded.

"Smelva. The skanky lunch lady in middle school. Remember her? Got her throat slashed in the alley behind Terry's."

Ginny thought of Smelva's dead body, her gaping neck. Tears leaked out of the corners of her eyes.

"Don't tell me you give a shit about that mean old bat. Remember how she used to make fun of … what was his name? The one with the thing?" Leilani gestured to her face. "They found someone else, too."

"Who?"

"Some scuzzy waitress down at Terry's. Throat slashed in her own apartment, like Smelva. It's on the news and everything." Leilani cackled. "'Both found in a pool of their own blood,'" she quoted, lingering on the word *blood*. She snapped her fingers. "Bernadette something-or-other. The po-po were sniffing around Terry's, collecting evidence or whatever."

Ginny remembered Bernie's lonely apartment, the gold necklace around her neck, the pleased look on her face. She hated Leilani.

"By the way, have you seen my necklace?"

Ginny ignored the question and pretended to sleep, waiting for Leilani to get bored and leave. She didn't have long to wait.

The world spun. Time passed. A clutter of doctors gathered outside her room.

"So, what can I tell her?" Dr. Zhou asked.

"Tell her she'll be fine," a female said. "We always tell the patients they're going to be fine."

Ginny kept her eyes closed, listening as they made their rounds.

The neurosurgeon, whose name eluded her, held court in the hallway outside her room.

"Her cranial pressure is back to normal," she said with imperious authority. "We can transfer her to step-down later this afternoon."

How many days had she been here? Ginny was not sure how they'd known to call Leilani, but it hurt her head too much to work it out. A monitor beeped, a high-pitched, steady rhythm. She closed her eyes.

Filthy cow.

She woke from more nightmares.

Dr. Zhou stood next to her bedside, hands in his pockets. He was staring at her.

"How are you?" he asked.

Ash Zhou. Another name on a very long list of people she had wronged. She should apologize, all the good it did Bernie.

"I'm sorry I was such a jerk," she blurted, before she changed her mind.

He cocked his head, his eyes quizzical.

"You know, in middle school. And—"

"Don't worry," he said. "Middle school was a long time ago." His birthmark crinkled at the edges, like tiny spider legs wiggling.

He lingered, his eyes narrowing. "Did you see anyone the night you were attacked?"

She hadn't. Didn't know who'd called the police.

The smell of burned matches. *Skank.* She couldn't even be certain that had been real.

There was no way she could admit to finding Smelva's dead body or going to Bernie's. With her record and reputation, they'd think she killed Bernie. And Smelva, too.

She needed to leave town. Start over. But where was she supposed to go? She'd spent all her money on booze and then, in a moment of weakness, given Bernie the only thing left of value. She had already pawned everything else.

A nurse whisked in to take her vitals, and Dr. Zhou scuttled away.

Ginny lay in bed, dozing fitfully, roused out of murky and unsettling dreams by voices in the hallway. Gray shadows oozed across the ceiling.

"Her scan is clear."

"We'll discharge her tomorrow. Her cranial pressure is normal and, other than persistent amnesia, she's fine. Neurologically, the patient is intact. Medicaid won't pay for another day in stepdown."

"Where will she go?"

"A question for Social Services."

Ginny didn't hear the rest. Social Services were likely the same people that ran public housing. She couldn't stand the thought of going back to her dank apartment with Leilani. But a burnout with no place to go—they would institutionalize her in some low-level residency facility with all the other suicidal fuckups and dried-out drunks with nowhere to go.

It would be Fishersville all over again.

Ginny had never been homeless, but Westhaven was only one step away. Public housing was full of transients. Everyone stuck in a kind of holding pattern on their way to someplace different or, worse, jail or the hospital.

Or the morgue.

No one ever made it out to something better, which was super fucking depressing. Even old Melva had wound up homeless at the end. Tears welled, and her throat felt thick. She wanted to do better. Be better. She did not want to wind up in Fishersville again.

Or, worse, dead with her throat slashed.

"You could stay at my place. Until you get back on your feet." Dr. Zhou leaned against the windowsill, arms folded across his chest.

"What's the catch?" she asked, wary.

"No catch. I have a studio apartment above the garage. I plan to rent it out at some point." Dr. Zhou gazed out the window before turning back to her. "It's empty right now. A filthy cow like you could stay until you find another place."

His voice was faint. An insect scuttling.

"What did you say?"

"I said you could stay until you find another place."

He was so earnest.

Her mind must be playing tricks again.

"Listen. I'm going to be straight up. I can't pay rent. And until I get my check from my last job, I can't even afford a packet of ramen." She tore the cotton tape from where the nurse had placed it after yanking out her IV and balled it up.

Dr. Zhou held out his hand, then threw it in the trash.

Ginny knew she would fuck things up. Get drunk and shoot her mouth off. Or some variation of inappropriate behavior. She'd gone from Gigi the Golden Girl to unemployed and penniless. *Skank. Cow.* People had told her she was a whore or bitch so many times, the terms had begun to sound like official diagnoses.

Dr. Zhou was still talking. "Sounds like poor impulse control, anger outbursts, with a dash of alcoholism thrown in." He raised his eyebrows and cocked his head. "I bet you're a vodka kind of gal."

Ginny froze. "What?"

Dr. Zhou said, "I was saying alcohol and drug dependency is common in people trying to cope with an underlying disorder or history of trauma." He paused. "You'd benefit from counseling or some kind of therapy." He stared at her. It was as if he could see through to her beating heart. It was a long speech, but he said it so matter-of-factly, she couldn't call him an asshole or judgmental prick like she had when her previous AA sponsor had suggested the same thing.

"Think on it. The team is still working on your discharge papers."

Her bladder was full. Bloated like a tick, her eyes puffy, her fingers swollen from the intravenous fluids.

Down the hall, monitors bleated, alarms ricocheted. What had once been a calm respite, a refuge, her sanctuary from the outside world, had become an ocean of noise. It made her seasick. Like being in the middle of happy hour, but on the floor, laid out, puke-drunk, dress hiked up to her panties, everyone gawking, stepping over her, drinks sloshing and dripping on her face.

She had been that girl in the middle of the floor more than once. And she felt like her now. Punch drunk, woozy.

The boy with the spider tattoo was offering her a way out.

"I'll do it," she finally said.

"I was hoping you'd say yes." He smiled.

She followed Dr. Zhou up the narrow stairs to the apartment over the garage. Through a window above the kitchen sink, the sky throbbed yellow, the sun a low orange ball on the horizon. It was the golden hour, when the whole world was afire.

When she glanced at Dr. Zhou to thank him yet again, he was staring at her. His amber-speckled irises reflected the slant of light and seemed to glow.

Despite the heat, Ginny shivered.

"Oh, I got something for you." He pulled a small box from his pocket and handed it to her. "Think of it as a get-well present."

As she ran her finger over the blue silky fabric, she heard a familiar, silken voice.

You're nothing but a smelly skank.

Her heart galloped. But when she raised her eyes, Dr. Zhou was smiling.

"Go on," he said, nodding at the box.

She hesitated, filled with an inexplicable dread. When she pried the lid open, she detected a faint scent of burned match.

Inside was a necklace, the gold chains splayed apart like Smelva's legs. With trembling hands, she picked it up and held it against the sunbeams streaming in from the window. A gold and jade Capricorn pendant swayed, sending a dazzling prism of golden light dancing.

Dr. Zhou leaned close. "I think it suits you," he whispered into her ear. "Don't you agree, Gigi?"

A Slippery Slope

By Leah St. James

"Here you go. Careful with her."

Karl Johnson turned to pass Kaylee the cornhusk doll. His heart stuttered. A balding man stood where she should be, waiting while Karl paid for the souvenir.

"Kaylee?" He'd dropped her hand for mere seconds to get his wallet.

He twisted toward the guy. "Did you see my daughter?"

"No, sorry."

The guy tried to move forward, but Karl blocked him. "Blond five-year-old wearing green antlers? She was here a second ago."

"Like I said, no." The guy pushed around Karl to get to the clerk.

"Kaylee?" Karl shouted her name, panic cementing in his chest. He rose to his toes to see over the crowd and shouted again.

Dozens of people filled the sidewalk and cobblestone street beyond. They'd descended on Colonial Williamsburg for its annual holiday fireworks celebration à la pre-Revolutionary America. All were in party mode, laughing and talking, bundled in layers to ward off the coldest night of the season.

But there wasn't a puffy pink parka in sight. Not one little blond girl in neon-green antlers.

She was…gone. Grabbed by someone?

A bolt of terror staggered him.

He shoved through the crowds, shouting his daughter's name.

Someone grabbed his arm from behind. He whipped around to face a sheriff's deputy.

"Thank God. Help me. I've lost my daughter."

Thirty minutes later, Karl stared at the flat, battleship-gray walls of the interview room at the local police headquarters, his heart still revving like a plane gearing for takeoff. If he were honest with himself, he'd been expecting his life to go off the rails. He just hadn't known when.

His hands trembled, making the mug of coffee he held clatter against the scarred wooden table. The table, utilitarian in material and design, looked and felt like a prop on the set of a 1940s noir movie. The only thing missing was the hard-boiled detective threatening to throw him in the slammer if he didn't cooperate.

"Mr. Johnson?"

His head snapped up. Enter the detective, although this one was a far cry from the one he'd imagined. Young, maybe in her early thirties, she had exotic eyes and blue-black hair that bounced in coils around a face the color of caramel.

She settled in the chair across from him, and a light floral scent floated toward him. Clearing her throat, she opened a folder on the table. Inside were a handful of pages, presumably pertaining to the search for his daughter.

"I'm Detective Marybeth Russo from the Virginia State Police, Bureau of Criminal Investigations. I have every hope of locating your daughter quickly."

He stifled the curse hovering on the tip of his tongue. "I appreciate your trying to inject optimism into this situation, Detective Russo, but forgive me if I don't share it. Can you even imagine what I'm thinking right now? My daughter is five years old, the perfect target for some perverted—" He chopped off the words before the primal scream that was building inside him could erupt.

The detective swallowed, but her expression betrayed nothing. "I assure you, Mr. Johnson, we are doing everything in our power to find Kaylee. We've issued an AMBER Alert and have a team of twenty conducting a grid search. On-site security are questioning shopkeepers and others in attendance. Chances are she wandered off and simply got lost."

"Kaylee wouldn't wander." He knew that to be true, even as he hoped Russo was right. "If she *did* get lost, she knows my cell number, and she's been taught to look for a police officer or someone in charge."

"Children don't always do what their parents tell them to do." The detective glanced at her notes. "Your description of Kaylee's clothing is helpful."

Karl snorted. He'd spent the afternoon gluing glitter and rhinestones to the pink rubber boots and antler headband, yet no one in the crowd had noticed her.

"But I need your help to narrow down the search."

Tension curled through his gut. He forced himself to sip from the cup of now cold and bitter brew. "I've already told the sheriff's deputy everything."

"And now you can tell me."

"To make sure I didn't do something with—or to—my daughter?"

She tipped her head, an acknowledgment that he was as much a suspect as anyone. Maybe at the top of the list.

Sitting back in the metal chair, he met Russo's eyes. "Kaylee and I arrived at the historic area around seven. We walked around, looked at the decorations, stopped and talked to actors in Colonial garb. Watched a performance by the fife and drum corps. We had about twenty minutes until the parade with Father Christmas when we stopped for a souvenir. I dropped her hand for one lousy minute to pay. That's when I … lost her."

It hurt to verbalize the words, like hacking up razors stuck in his throat.

A sharp rap on the door interrupted, and a uniformed officer poked his head through. "Detective?" Looking worried, he jerked his head to the side.

Sweat broke out on Karl's brow. When Russo tossed him a frown over her shoulder as she hurried out to consult with the officer, his heart picked up its thumping, nearly drowning out the *PleaseGodNo PleaseGodNo* chant echoing in his head.

When Russo rejoined him at the table, she held two plastic evidence bags—one containing a piece of paper and the other a couple of gaudy rhinestones… like the ones he'd glued onto Kaylee's boots.

He shot his hand forward to grab the bag with the note, but Russo was quicker. She extended her palm in a be-patient gesture that made Karl want to punch the wall. Her eyes fell to the note and came back to him. "Who is Amanda?"

And there it was, the reason his life had gone off the rails.

Memories flooded him, flinging him to that moment six years earlier when they'd met. The blond, blue-eyed, twentysomething vice president of a local women's motorcycle club had looked more beauty contestant than biker.

The topper was her wise-ass personality, which made him feel alive. She'd opened her mouth to give someone sass, and his heart had sunk to his knees before rebounding into his chest. It had never fully settled.

"Mr. Johnson?" Russo's voice jerked him back to the present. "Who is Amanda?"

He swallowed the spit that had pooled in his mouth. "My ex-wife."

She frowned. "According to your statement to the deputy, Kaylee's mother is 'out of the picture.' What does that mean?"

Gripping his hands together under the table, he forced a few shallow breaths. "We divorced almost a year ago in California. I got full custody, and Kaylee and I moved here. Kaylee hasn't seen her since."

Before the detective could follow up, he tipped his chin to the evidence bag. "The note's from her, isn't it? May I see it?"

She squinted at him, then passed him the bag.

His eyes devoured the words like a starving man at a banquet: *Midnight at Sarah's Creek Marina.* It was signed *Amanda.*

His insides turned to ice. "Where did you get this?"

"A woman turned it over to one of the local cops."

"What woman?"

"My turn, Mr. Johnson. If your ex-wife took Kaylee, why would she want to meet? Why wouldn't she simply take her and run?" She leaned back with her arms crossed, her eyes mere slits. "Maybe your story is a lie. Maybe Amanda is Kaylee's custodial parent. Maybe it was you who snatched Kaylee and fled."

"I have full custody," he snapped.

"That should be easy for me to verify." She tapped her pen against the folder, her gaze focused on him, as if she dared him to deny her.

"Detective, once you locate Kaylee and she's safe, I'll be happy to answer any questions and provide whatever documentation you need. But right now, Amanda has Kaylee. If we don't find her before midnight, my daughter's safety—"

His voice caught—the thoughts too terrible—and his words fell away.

Russo's eyebrows lifted. "Are you implying she's not safe with her mother?" She leaned forward, elbows on the table. "Explain."

The tension that had been building since Kaylee's disappearance erupted, and he slapped his palms on the table, making the mug rattle and her folder jump. "We're wasting time. We need to find Kaylee."

"So tell me why your ex-wife took her."

He let out a breath. "Amanda is using Kaylee as bait, to get to me."

Russo didn't quite roll her eyes, but it was close. "For what reason? She wants you back?"

Whispering a curse under his breath, he folded his hands on the table and decided how many of his beans he wanted to spill. "She wants to kill me."

Russo's mouth twisted into a smirk. "Really. Your ex-wife travels from California to Virginia and kidnaps your daughter so she can kill you? On a believability scale, that's about a two out of ten."

"I don't care what you believe, as long as you find my daughter." He pointed to the clock on the wall. "And you're running out of time."

Russo pushed a yellow legal pad and a pen toward him. "I need a list of your ex-wife's friends and relatives who might have knowledge of her whereabouts and plans. When you're done, you can go home. We'll take it from there."

"I'll be at the marina at midnight."

"No. I can't have you anywhere near there, especially if your life is in danger, as you claim." She shoved her chair back, the legs screeching in protest. "I'll be back for the list."

As the door closed behind her, Karl opened his contacts to a list of names he thought he'd never need again and began writing. A moment later, his phone buzzed. Jon Malloy, the friend who'd introduced him to Amanda.

His heart leapt as he jabbed at the *ANSWER* button. Before Jon could speak, he said, "Amanda's here."

"Already?" Jon groaned. "She and her parents were released yesterday. The governor commuted their sentences—thanks to a big campaign donation. I was hoping to catch you in time, so you could take precautions."

"Too late. I can't figure out how she found me."

"Driver's license, I imagine. Money buys information."

"I've been stupid, but no more." Russo might have instructed him to run home and hide, but he'd be damned if he'd sit by while they searched for Kaylee. "I'm going home to grab some things"—namely, his registered handgun—"then back out to look for them." He sucked back a breath. "One way or another, my ex and I will have the come-to-Jesus moment she seems to want."

He disconnected as the door whined open. When Russo stepped into the room, he pushed the legal pad toward her. "Contact info for Amanda's parents and several close friends, but don't expect them to help."

Frowning, Russo skimmed the list. "I guess you're not their favorite person?"

"More like the enemy."

Her deadpan cop's stare sent a cold shiver through him. She'd already decided he was the bad guy. "Okay, I'll bite. Why are you the enemy, and why does your ex want to kill you?" She eyed him as though he were a patient who'd escaped from a psych ward.

He choked back the urge to laugh. There was nothing funny about his ex or the reason she wanted him dead. "Amanda is the vice president of a women's motorcycle club in California. On the surface, they're a purely social and philanthropic group, well known and liked in the community. The family runs a legitimate shipping company that employs a lot of people in the area—more good will—but it fronts their real business."

"Let me guess," she said, words slow and mocking, "drugs and guns. You were one of the male biker groupies, got so offended when you found out the sad truth that you took Kaylee and ran, and now they want you dead?"

He swallowed a curse. "Hardly. I was the new deputy sheriff in town who got suckered into believing the fantasy, married the heiress, had a kid, then discovered the family secret."

She shook her head. "Not buying it. In your statement, you said you're a carpenter."

"I am now. I changed careers when we moved here. No taste for the law anymore."

Her fingers tapped the table. "The bigger question: why would someone running a criminal enterprise marry a cop?"

He returned his version of the cop's stare. "Insurance."

"Ah…they got their own personal protection cop in the family."

"They thought they did. I played along after reporting what I knew to the Feds."

Her eyebrows jackknifed. "You turned your wife and her parents in?"

"Turned them in, wore a wire, and testified at trial. I put them in jail." He recounted his earlier call with Jon, the reason they had been released from prison.

Russo shook her head. "Damn, Johnson, that's harsh. You did that to me, I might want to kill you, too."

Her words rang in his head for most of the long drive to his home near the western shore of Chesapeake Bay. Turning evidence on his wife had been hard. But over the years, Amanda's sass had turned to a viciousness toward anyone who went against her. It had frightened him, and that was *before* he discovered she was in the business of selling death. He wanted nothing to do with her blood money. More importantly, he wanted Kaylee far from that life.

Head pounding with the painful memories, he pulled to a stop in front of his cottage. He rushed up the porch two steps at a time, his mind on the task ahead. Get his gun. Find his daughter.

As he unlocked the door, a metallic *click-click* tore into the silence. Karl froze for a heartbeat, then dropped to the porch.

Inches to his right, the door frame splintered.

He dove inside the house, taking cover behind a sofa.

Shots shattered the wood frame. An acrid combination of charcoal and sulfur scented the air.

Karl doubled in on himself, visualizing his home's layout while his mind struggled with the knowledge that Amanda had outplayed him. Again.

His heart thundered. He breathed deeply, trying to calm it. "You wanted to talk, Amanda. Here I am."

Close by, a floorboard creaked.

"Why are you doing this?"

"Because she wants you dead. And I want what she wants."

His heart skipped. "Jon?" He almost popped his head over the couch to confirm what his ears had registered.

The overhead light came on, and he shut his eyes against the brightness while his brain scrambled for a coherent thought. Footsteps closed in. He crab-walked around the side of the couch.

"Where's Kaylee?"

A shot exploded inches away. He fumbled for his phone and hit 911.

"She's safe with her mother. They dropped me here an hour ago. Could be anywhere by now."

"Meaning the marina was a decoy. Where are you meeting them?"

Jon laughed, a sinister sound. "Nice try. But unlike you, I'm not ratting on Amanda."

Realization hit him hard, and Karl swallowed a wave of humiliation. "How long have you been sleeping with her?"

"Since the beginning. We both thought you'd find out, but you're too trusting, buddy."

"You suckered me from the start. Why?"

"Amanda had plans to ramp up the club's not-so-public activity. The local cops were turning a blind eye, to a point, thanks to continued contributions to the benevolent fund, but we needed a patsy. Then you took the deputy's job, new to town, no friends or family. So needy." He paused, his footsteps coming closer. "We wanted to draw you into the organization slowly, so you'd be implicated if things went south. But when you fell so hard for Amanda, we couldn't let the opportunity pass."

"I'm glad I could play along with your scheme." After a beat, he said, "Amanda lured Kaylee from my side tonight, didn't she?"

Jon's chuckle made his stomach churn. "You made it so easy. Never spotted us tailing you from your house to Williamsburg. You were standing at the edge of the crowd, your attention on the clerk at the counter. Amanda crouched down about ten feet away, and when Kaylee looked our way, she ran straight to her mother, not another thought for you."

Heat crept up Karl's chest at how easily he'd allowed this to happen. And if he made another mistake, he'd be dead.

Taking a chance, he peeked over the sofa's arm.

Jon stood above him, pointing the nose of a 9mm Beretta at his head.

Karl lifted his arms in a don't-shoot gesture. "You're no cold-blooded killer, Jon. Even for Amanda."

Jon's laugh sent chills up Karl's spine. He braced, prepared to run.

The front door slammed against its jamb.

"Police! Drop your weapon!" Russo shouted, barricaded behind the door.

Jon pivoted, his weapon spitting out multiple rounds.

Russo stepped out and fired three quick bursts.

Jon staggered and turned a shocked gaze to Karl before collapsing, a bloody pool spreading beneath him.

Russo hurried forward, her weapon aimed at Jon's body. She glanced at Karl. "You hit?"

"No." Karl stood, wiping sweat from his brow. "You?"

She shook her head and holstered her weapon. "I was on my way here and heard the 911 call. I guess your ex *does* want to kill you."

"And she still has Kaylee." He gestured toward the body. "He knew where they are."

"Who is he?"

"My ex-best friend, who was banging my ex-wife. Apparently, he was willing to kill for her."

"Your story just keeps getting better, Johnson." She slipped on gloves and reached into Jon's pocket for his phone. "I'm betting he has your ex in his call list."

Karl grimaced while she pointed the phone at Malloy's face to unlock it, then punched a few commands. After a moment, the speaker came to life, ringing another phone.

Russo held it up for Karl to hear.

"Is it done?" Amanda's voice was breathless, excited.

Nausea roiled his gut. "Not quite. Jon missed. I'm alive and well. Surprise!"

Dead silence, then, "Where is he?"

"The police are dealing with him." No way was he going to reveal that her lover was dead.

Curses flew from her mouth.

"Just tell me where Kaylee is, and I promise I won't press charges for taking her." He scowled as he spit out the lie. "Are you at the marina?"

"Wouldn't you like to know?"

Russo circled her hand. *Keep her talking.*

Frustrated, he gave his ex the groveling he knew she would want to hear. "It's not too late to make things right. You don't have to take the blame for what Jon did."

"Is that Daddy? I want Daddy!" Kaylee's voice screeched across the transmission.

"Kaylee!" He grabbed for the phone, but Russo yanked it back. Curling his fingers into a fist, he said, "Don't be scared, baby. I'm coming."

The sound of scuffling from the other end froze him. It muffled quickly, as if Amanda had covered the mouthpiece. A moment later, she said, "We're done, Karl." Her tone was flat, dull, and it terrified him. "Good-bye."

"Wait! Don't hang up!" His brain scrambled for the right words. "I'm begging you, bring Kaylee back. She just started kindergarten. She's making friends. Don't pull her away from her new life. Now that you're out, I'll make sure you're part of her life. I promise."

More lies, slipping so easily off his tongue. Maybe that's how a life in crime starts, one little lie at a time.

It took Amanda a count of ten to respond. "You think I'll fall for your scout act again? But to prove I'm not as heartless as you, I'll let you and Kaylee say goodbye. Meet me at the marina. You have ten minutes before Kaylee and I take off for our new life without you."

The call disconnected, and Karl lunged for the door. Glaring, Russo stepped in front of him. "No way I let you walk into that trap. Backup's on the way. Let us do our job."

Their gazes locked, and Karl shifted back. "You're the boss."

When she nodded and turned to speak to a uniform, he bolted from the house.

Russo swore and yelled for him to stop.

He jumped in his vehicle and tore down the driveway, gravel spitting behind him.

Russo tailed him down the winding streets. Five minutes later, Karl skidded onto the marina property. Russo pulled up behind him.

The moon was new, throwing dim light, and fog drifted off the water. Twenty-five feet away, a red sedan sat at the boathouse under a weak spotlight, exhaust spewing from its tailpipe. The interior was dark, but a shadow moved against the glass. Kaylee? Amanda?

He stepped from his vehicle, hands up. "I'm here, Amanda! Where's Kaylee?"

Russo scrambled behind her door, weapon drawn. "Do you have a death wish, Johnson?" She spoke quietly, but her voice echoed off the fog.

"You brought the cops with you?" Amanda's voice came from the right, across the lot from the sedan. "Not smart, Karl."

He spun, squinting into the murkiness. "Not my idea." He inched forward. "Where's Kaylee?"

A shot fired, piercing his front windshield. He dove behind his car door and reached for his weapon, remembering too late that he'd never retrieved it.

Russo shouted, "Police! Drop the weapon, Amanda, before your daughter is hurt. We'll all go back to the station and talk this out."

Amanda bolted into view and raced for the sedan, firing shots in their direction.

Russo zigzagged forward, her weapon drawn.

The sedan's back window lowered a fraction. A tiny arm waved from the opening. "Daddy!"

"Don't shoot!" His voice cracked. "Kaylee's in that car!" He dove into his vehicle and started the engine.

The red sedan leapt forward, careening toward the street. Karl pulled out behind it, praying for control, for wisdom, knowing he had neither at that moment.

He followed down the village's waterfront street, cruising past darkened businesses. Amanda was pulling ahead, but he feared pushing her faster. She wouldn't get far before hitting the water.

Russo joined the parade, her emergency lights throwing red and blue bolts like an out-of-control disco ball.

Amanda accelerated around a curve, toward a bridge that was under construction. Her taillights disappeared into the fog.

Sweat dripped into Karl's eyes as he struggled to focus.

There, just ahead. Taillights. They fishtailed, and the lights went airborne.

There was a crash, and Karl's heart stopped. He slammed on his brakes and fell from his car.

The sedan had gone head-first over the railing and dangled dizzily toward the creek. Thirty feet below, rapids hissed and bubbled.

The interior was dark. Silent. The driver's airbag had deployed, but there was no movement.

He grabbed the rear door handle and tugged. Locked.

Russo rushed up, breathless. "I've called for backup."

Ignoring her, he yelled, "Kaylee! Can you hear me?"

Something moved inside, and the car took a sickening lurch toward the water. Pulling on the handle, Karl leaned against the weight and threw a panicked glance to Russo. "It's going over!"

She grabbed the other handle. They planted their feet, pulling against gravity until the balance steadied.

A shadow moved inside. "Kaylee? Lower the window!"

"Daddy?" Her voice was thin and shaky, and it had never sounded more beautiful. After an eon, the window lowered, and he yanked his little girl to safety.

She sobbed, her face pressed into his chest, and mumbled something about being sorry for leaving him and running to Mommy.

"Everything's okay, baby."

Metal ripped against metal as the sedan dropped another foot toward the water.

He set Kaylee down, brushing powder from her face and hair.

He turned to the car. Tendrils of Russo's hair had plastered against her face, and she grunted, her feet staggering forward with the car's weight.

Karl thrust his arm through the open window, hoping for leverage. "I'll try to hang on. Take Kaylee. Don't let her watch."

Russo let go and bent over, hands on her thighs, gulping air. She reached for Kaylee's hand. "Come with me, sweetheart. Your daddy will be right with you."

Karl peered inside the vehicle. Amanda's head lolled. She moaned.

He twisted to reach her and shook her shoulder. The car lurched.

She jerked upright. Shrieking, she scrambled to her knees, seesawing the car toward the water.

He fumbled to grab her hands, wrists crossed, much as they had on their wedding day. He forced the image from his mind and pulled. The muscles in his arms and legs screamed.

The car dipped again, its frame groaning.

Amanda whimpered. "Kaylee?"

"Safe."

"Jon?"

"Dead." He had no energy to soften the blow.

Pain washed over her face. "I wish I'd never married you."

He was trying to decide how to respond when she added, "Kaylee isn't even yours. She's Jon's. We wanted to be together. You're supposed to be dead."

His breath left him as his gut sensed the truth. They'd played him the fool again.

Sirens wailed in the distance. Help on the way.

He glanced back. Russo had turned Kaylee's back to the scene.

His grip on Amanda loosened, their hands slick with sweat. The car dipped, pulling him forward.

Their eyes met, hers cold and hate-filled. She'd never give up until he was out of their lives forever.

Wondering if he'd have the strength to do what was needed, he said, "Kaylee might not share my blood, but she'll always be my daughter. You lost your chance, Amanda. Goodbye."

Her eyes flared. Panicked, she tried to inch closer. "You wouldn't!"

"I'd do anything to protect Kaylee from the life you've chosen."

"No!"

He inhaled a huge breath and ripped himself free of her grasp. Stumbling backward, he watched, only half horrified, as the car somersaulted into the water, bobbing in the rapids before sinking below the surface.

Moments later, as he hugged Kaylee, vowing to never fail her again, he thought about the division between right and wrong, the slippery slope that greased its path.

Some might say he'd chosen the wrong path. But then, one person's crime was another's punishment.

It Ain't Over 'Til It's Over

By Mary Dutta

"We're *this* close to the finish line," Deborah Holt said, holding her fuchsia-tipped fingers scant millimeters apart. She had adopted a lot of sports metaphors since starting Charlottesville's host-city bid for the People's Games. *Full-court press. Cover all bases. Move the ball forward.* The lingo spilled across the posters arrayed on easels around the meeting room. *Go for the Gold! One Team, One Dream! For Love of the Game! Go the Distance!* The slogans varied, but Deborah's image appeared on every poster, posed in local sports venues with an assortment of balls, sticks, nets, and in every photo at least one green accessory—their signature bid color, a shade chosen no doubt to bring out her eyes.

Deputy Mayor Scott Howell had given up hoping that she would throw in the towel. He wondered what slang expressions she would have used if she'd settled on some other event to rebrand Charlottesville. A folk fair, maybe, or a pimento cheese festival. Either affectation might have been preferable to the locker-room-pep-talk-speak she'd spouted since deciding to bid on hosting the Games.

"American history is as passé as leather helmets," Deborah said. "We need to sell fun, action, excitement. First, we knock the selection-committee site visit out of the park. Then the People's Games are going to put Charlottesville on the global map."

Scott had never understood how an off-brand Olympics could be anything but a money loser, especially when sports fans could simply travel a couple of hours up the road and cheer on DC's professional sports teams.

He thought—not for the first or even the thousandth time—that the city *should* have adopted his own idea of a theater festival. They had the target audience. They had the venues. He had gotten buy-in from Charlottesville Opera and the American Shakespeare Center over in Staunton, not to mention the free labor available from neighboring community-theater stalwarts thrilled at the chance to mingle with their professional brethren. Several vineyards had expressed interest in tie-in packages. And he'd sourced solid data for all his projections on the bump in hotel, restaurant, and retail revenue a festival would bring.

As far as Scott could tell, Deborah had built *her* proposal in some sort of fantasy league. The expenses for the hosting bid had already snowballed even more wildly than her over-optimistic claims of how much money the Games would bring into the community. For a director of economic development, she had a shockingly tenuous grasp of economics. He shuddered to think what further damage she could do as mayor, a job she was obviously angling for.

That shortcoming did not seem to bother the other city employees at the meeting, who greeted her every bullet point with rapturous approval. "Put me in, coach," said a woman in a green *Back the Bid* T-shirt. At least Deborah's picture wasn't on that. The remark elicited chuckles around the room. Even Andrew Lilly, the city's dour CFO, mustered a tight-lipped grin.

Scott had not managed to rally similar support for his festival plan, his opposition to the bid, or his nascent mayoral campaign. If only he could get Mayor Armstrong's backing, he wouldn't care about Deborah and her cheerleaders. But lately, the mayor was giving a lot more attention to her and the Games than he was to his loyal deputy. This despite all the years Scott had skillfully handled everything from the Foxfield Races to UVA fraternities, working overtime to keep a close eye on city finances and long-range goals, so the mayor could devote himself to cutting ribbons and handing out keys to the city. Scott had been on deck too long to let someone else steal his chance to step up to the plate as Armstrong's successor.

Deborah wrapped up her presentation to enthusiastic applause. "Any questions?"

"How far over budget is the bid?" Scott said, ignoring the raised eyebrows and rolled eyes that rippled around the conference table. The woman in the *Bid* shirt snorted.

"We're not exactly in line with our original budget," Deborah said, with a breezy wave of dismissal, "but once I dug into the city's finances, I found some underutilized accounts we can tap into. Andrew's been a big help with that."

In Scott's experience, the CFO held onto the city's money like it was coming out of his own pocket. Early on, Andrew had shared Scott's concern over the risk the city was taking by investing so heavily in a bid that might come to nothing or, worse, succeed and then do irreparable damage to the city coffers when the Games proved to be a bust. But if he'd let her root through his precious accounts, then apparently Andrew had joined Team Deborah.

"Sounds like things are under control," Mayor Armstrong said, standing and signaling the end of the meeting. He escorted Deborah toward the door.

Scott hustled to catch up with him. "Could I have a quick word?"

The mayor paused as Deborah walked on. "This isn't about that theater thing again, is it?"

"I'm thinking this might be a good time to announce my candidacy and your endorsement," Scott said in a rush, trying not to focus on his boss's *Back the Bid* lapel pin. "We want to get out ahead of the whole bid-announcement distraction." He could wait until he was elected to realize his theatrical ambitions.

The mayor glanced around at the posters, Deborah's green eyes twinkling back at him from every direction. "Let's wait until after the bid," he said. "We don't want to steal anyone's thunder."

Scott watched him walk away with a sinking feeling that it was not *his* thunder that was being protected. If a successful bid for the People's Games caused the mayor to throw his support to Deborah, Scott's campaign to succeed him was doomed before it even began. The selection-committee site visit was in two weeks, which meant Scott had fourteen days to ensure the failure of Charlottesville's bid and any mayoral aspirations Deborah might harbor.

He hurried back to his desk, brainstorming ways to make that happen, but slowed at the sound of voices in the supply closet. Peering through the partially open door, he saw Andrew and Deborah huddled between the jumbo toilet paper rolls and a teetering pile of binders.

"You're the one who wanted to keep secrets," Deborah said.

Andrew started to answer, then held up a hand and turned toward the door. Apparently, the two of them were sharing a lot more than financial files.

Virginia really is for lovers, thought Scott, as he hotfooted it to his office. An affair would undoubtedly explain the married CFO's uncharacteristic support for Deborah's free-spending ways. And their sudden closeness.

A moment later, Deborah stuck her head in. "Got a minute, Scotty?" Nobody called him Scotty. Her attempt at intimacy was as phony as her veneers. She seated herself without being asked, smoothing her green silk scarf and taking a deep breath. "You know, Scotty, there's no I in team," she said.

There's no I in mayor, either, Scott thought. And since the election would take place well before the Games, Deborah would be firmly ensconced in the city's highest office before everyone learned that Scott had been right all along about what a bad idea they were.

"Ah, we're batting a thousand?" he said.

Deborah pointed at him. "Exactly. It doesn't matter if you win or lose, it's how you play the game. But we're in it to win it. And that means I can't have you sitting on the bench."

Scott struggled to come up with an answering sports cliché, but she was already heading out, probably to take a victory lap around City Hall.

Scott played the game as best he could: slow-walking requests for facility repairs, entangling orders for local goods in red tape. He even found a UVA economics professor who was happy to pen an editorial on the riskiness of the bid in exchange for a building permit for a she shed in her backyard. But his best efforts were trampled under the blitz of Deborah's ambition.

In the home stretch before the site visit, he made frantic rounds of the city's business and civic organizations, dashing from Masons to Kiwanis to the Chamber of Commerce. He warned them the Games would take more away from the community than they would add, reminded them of the huge financial holes that hosting cities had dug themselves over the years. The organizers would bring in their own vendors and flood the market with souvenir goods made overseas, undercutting local peddlers of apple butter and Founding Father tchotchkes. "You should ask some hard questions when they come to town," he said. "Let them know you're not pushovers."

"Look, Scott, we're all businesspeople here," one Rotarian said during a breakfast meeting. "We know sometimes you have to spend money to make money. But Deborah seems to have everything under control. And I hear Andrew has run the numbers, and even he's on board now."

Scott left the meeting weighed down by pancakes and thwarted plans. As he trudged back to the Downtown Mall parking lot, he noticed the couple in the vehicle idling next to him at a stoplight. Andrew and Deborah? Were they rolling out of bed and into work together now? Before he could reach out and knock on the car window, the light turned green, and they drove away.

Scott could not compete with whatever Andrew was getting from Deborah and didn't care to imagine what exactly it might be. He needed to find a way to block their offense, but for now, he had to focus on his next meeting with Charlottesville's Block the Bid Coalition.

He soon discovered that Deborah had beaten him to the punch. "The director of economic development met with us and addressed all our concerns," the coalition's chair told him. "She promised that a lot of the money that comes in from the Games will be directed toward our priorities."

"But people in your group chat still seem upset," Scott said.

The woman shrugged. "Pretty much the only one who posts on the chat anymore is somebody calling himself BidBan."

BidBanner, Scott mentally corrected her. He should have thought to use more than one alias in the chat, but he had assumed he'd be swamped by the sheer number of other posters.

"Anyway, we've disbanded," the chair said. "Deborah promised to run interference with the mayor's office on how the profits from the Games are allotted."

Scott knew when he had been beaten. He didn't waste time trying to convince the woman that there would be no profits. She would just have to take it on the chin when she realized Deborah had fumbled the ball.

As the clock ticked down to the selection-committee visit, Scott saw more and more *Back the Bid* shirts and fewer and fewer options. A negative online review of Deborah's performance at her previous job in Norfolk produced a surge of hope, until he remembered he had posted it himself in an earlier attempt to undermine her plans. Late one night, he ordered some spray paint, but in the light of day, his plan to scrawl anti-bid graffiti on Monticello seemed as preposterous as his wild ideas on how to eliminate his rival permanently.

At work, Deborah held court, the mayor avoided him, and Scott hunkered down in his office. When the site visit finally arrived, Deborah and her supporters squired the committee members around to showcase the city. Scott added a running tally of the cost of the meals and hotels and entertainment to the already dire financials surrounding the bid. He was paying attention to the city's money, even if Andrew had dropped the ball. Deborah could have saved a fortune, for instance, by taking the visitors to Michie Tavern and passing it off as local culture. Not to mention the gift bags. She might as well have stuffed them with cash.

His nerves began to fray with the effort of maintaining the delicate balance between advancing his own plan to undermine the bid and keeping in the mayor's good graces by seeming to support it. He reluctantly put on his game face and showed up at an all-hands-on-deck reception at a local vineyard. The location was particularly painful, given that it was one of the places he had worked with on his theater plans. He still had the mockup of the pamphlet promoting their wine tastings: *A Taste of the Theater.* He gripped his wine glass so tightly at the memory that the stem snapped.

Scott looked around to see if anyone had noticed, but only Andrew, who stood silently next to Deborah, was watching. Deborah gestured at Scott like she was using hand signals to call plays. Eventually, he realized she was urging him to mingle. He grabbed another glass of wine and forced himself to join the party.

"The university stadium is quite impressive," he overheard a woman say.

"Isn't it?" he said, inserting himself between her and her companion. "Although I don't believe they've ever made it available for anyone else's sporting events." He continued to make the rounds, slipping deniable dissuasion into every conversation.

"I hear the people of Bordeaux are more enthusiastic about the Games than the people of Charlottesville," he said to a man with an unidentifiable accent. "And, of course, they have that wonderful wine." He took a gulp of his cabernet franc and winced, then excused himself. On his way out, he made sure to nod at the mayor, hoping all his pass fakes had convinced him of Scott's sincerity.

On the final day of the visit, Scott arrived at the last minute to join the ceremonial presentation of the bid at John Paul Jones Arena, only because the mayor expected everyone to attend. Green balloons filled the loge. The Jumbotron flashed the *Back the Bid* logo. NBC29 stood ready to capture the moment. The only thing missing was Deborah, and no way was she sitting this one out.

As the time for the official bid presentation approached, the committee members began to check their phones and murmur among themselves. The mayor ran low on small talk. One of Deborah's cheerleaders circulated among the sea of green T-shirts, trying to pump up the fading energy of the crowd.

"Just picture it," she said, taking a position in front of the balcony railing and gesturing at the space behind her. "The crowds, the excitement. The—"

She leaned over the railing to peer at something below.

And screamed.

People rushed to the railing, more screams ringing out. The crowd surged around Scott, carrying him forward to the source of the commotion. Two levels below, he saw Deborah's body splayed across the seats. She was down for the count. Forever.

Mayor Armstrong, green tie askew, ushered the selection committee toward the exit, a protective arm flung out to shepherd them through the chaos. "Where the hell have you been?" he snarled at Scott as he passed.

Scott looked up from where Deborah lay and spied Andrew sitting above it all in an upper section of the arena. The CFO smiled his tight-lipped smile as Scott climbed the stairs.

"That railing is too high for her to have just fallen over," Scott said. "Someone must have pushed her."

Andrew nodded. "The police will probably be wondering if she had any enemies."

"A scorned lover, perhaps?"

"Not me," Andrew said. "I'm a happily married man."

"Right," Scott said. "I figured all that secrecy had to be about something else. Is that how Deborah bought your support for the bid—by blackmailing you with what she found when she went poking around in the city's finances? That you've been embezzling?"

Andrew stared down at the panicked crowd.

"You know, being deputy mayor is a thankless job," Scott said. "You have to oversee staff, operations—and, unfortunately for you, cashflow." He flipped down the seat next to Andrew and sat. "But it does have some advantages, like being able to track city employees' computer usage. So, while all the bid backers were blowing up balloons and distributing gift bags this morning, I was in the office, tracking Deborah's digital fingerprints straight to the incriminating evidence she found about you. Were you tired of buying her silence? Did you finally decide to shut her up for good?"

"Cool story," Andrew said, still focused on the scene below. "Now let me tell you one. You've been desperate to stop this bid to protect your dream of being mayor. A lot of people will testify to that. Maybe you figured the only way to put an end to the bid was to put an end to Deborah. And if you're guilty of murder, it wouldn't be hard to believe you're guilty of framing me for embezzlement to make it look like I had a motive to kill her."

The voices below grew more agitated.

"We've both been playing the long game," Scott said, "and Deborah threw us both a curveball."

"Looks like she lost the bid in sudden-death overtime," Andrew agreed. "The committee will never choose Charlottesville now. Bad publicity is an automatic red card."

The Jumbotron flashed the *Back the Bid* logo, then went black.

"It's definitely curtains for the People's Games," Andrew said.

"But the show must go on," Scott said, "and I've got a great idea waiting in the wings. My theater festival will bring in a lot of money, more than enough to replace any missing city funds."

Andrew nodded. "I guess you'll step into the role of mayor, now that Deborah's not going to be around to upstage you. Given the right support, of course."

They sat side-by-side, watching the escalating drama unfold.

"If we tell the police we were together all day," Andrew said at last, "then we're both in the clear." He got up and walked to the end of the row, and waited.

Scott sat a moment longer, running the possible plays in his head, then rose and joined him. He extended his fist, and Andrew bumped it with his own.

"Teamwork makes the dream work," Scott said.

Game Over

By Heather Weidner

Taking one more swig of her vanilla latte, Jocelyn Craig soaked in the last quiet moments before the city came alive. *Time for work.* She dropped her cup in the nearest trash can and took one last look at the Kanawha Canal, the narrow body of water that snaked through downtown Richmond next to the James River. This area, part thoroughfare and part park, was her serene spot before another hectic day of deadlines and rewrites.

A scream followed by several shouts disrupted her moment of Zen and sent her curiosity into overdrive. Hustling over, she found a small group lining the fencing that kept people from tumbling into the canal. A second shriek prompted Jocelyn to move closer.

"Somebody call 911," a man who'd scaled the waist-high fence said. "There's a guy floating in the water. Look down there."

"That's just trash. That's not a person," someone in the back said.

"Y'all stop recording this and call the police. There's someone floating face down," the first man said before he jumped in the canal, sending a plume of water into the air.

Since the crowd seemed more interested in capturing the event on video, Jocelyn pulled out her phone and connected with emergency dispatch.

"This is Jocelyn Craig with the *Richmond Sentinel.* I'm on the Canal Walk near Brown's Island. Someone spotted a person floating in the canal, and a guy jumped in to save him. Please send help."

"Is the person responsive?" the dispatcher asked.

"I don't think so. He's in a dead man's float," Jocelyn whispered.

"There are two bike units nearby, and the EMTs are about two minutes out."

"Thank you." Jocelyn disconnected and wormed her way to the front of the ever-growing crowd. Moments later, two officers leaned their bicycles against the wall and used the gate to access the steps as the Good Samaritan towed the lifeless body to the edge.

Jocelyn stepped closer to the stairs for a better look as both officers helped the guy out of the water and pulled the body onto the cement. Two EMTs raced down the steps.

Jocelyn tapped notes on her phone and snapped a few photos. She fired off a text to her editor about the unfolding situation.

Stay with it. See what it turns into, Eric, her editor, replied.

Jocelyn pocketed her phone and inched still closer.

After what seemed like an eternity, one of the officers climbed the stairs to talk to the rescuer. The officer said something Jocelyn didn't catch and moved into the crowd for witness statements. When everyone started to talk at once, Jocelyn took advantage of the chaos to slip over to the man who was trying in vain to squeeze the water out of his shorts.

"Excuse me. I know you're in a hurry, but I'm Jocelyn Craig with the *Richmond Sentinel.* Do you have a minute to answer a few questions?" She pulled a small notebook and pen from her purse and flipped to a blank page.

"Uh, I guess. It took me four seconds to tell the cop what I knew."

"Your name? And how did you come upon the victim?" she asked, launching into full reporter mode.

"Todd Reynolds. I noticed something in the water that looked weird. I mean, there are all kinds of things in the canal, but a guy in a tuxedo is pretty out of place."

"Did he look familiar?"

"Nope. I did hear the cop say he didn't have a wallet or phone on him. Kinda strange." Todd stomped both shoes, and Jocelyn stepped back to avoid the splash.

"Maybe they're at the bottom of the canal," Jocelyn said.

"Maybe." He shrugged. "That's all I know. I'll look for your article online. Make sure to mention I'm a freelance graphic designer." He jogged through the growing crowd.

Jocelyn stepped back and clicked her contact for the Richmond PD. The phone rang several times before a gruff said, "Hey, Josie. Whaddya want? I'm kinda up to my elbows in alligators here."

"C'mon, Karl, you're not too busy to chat with your favorite reporter, are you?" She paused for less than a beat. "I'll be quick. I was down at the canal enjoying my coffee when this guy fished a body out of the water. Can I get a copy of the report?"

"Sheesh, girl. The two beat cops haven't even finished at the scene," he said. "It may be late today before I can get hold of it."

"I know. I want to make sure I get one as soon as it's available. Pretty please."

"I gotcha covered. There's rumblings about a press conference later. Keep your ears open for that. I gotta run. There's another crisis brewing."

Before Jocelyn could comment, she realized he had already disconnected. Not wanting to waste time getting her car, she jog-walked the four blocks to her office. At her desk, she typed what she knew about the victim and looked through her pictures to see if any were usable. After she uploaded a couple that might pass, she sent what she had to her editor with a note about a follow-up after the presser. Knowing everything was hurry-up and wait in the world of reporting, Jocelyn then opened another file and reread a puff piece she'd written about a budding computer programmer who'd created a website mapping all the little free libraries in the area. She added a couple of commas and sent it over to Eric for review.

Jocelyn stretched, trying to ward off the groggies. Her caffeine addiction won out over her better judgment about office coffee, and she padded down the hall to the kitchenette. An acrid smell permeated the air around the coffee station. Someone had left the empty coffee pot on the burner of the ancient machine. She put the pot in the sink and flicked off the orange button. "So much for that idea," she said to no one and found a Coke in the back.

Her phone alerted her to the arrival of an email. Karl had come through. Jocelyn scanned the brief police report, but it didn't contain any new details. The email did include a note that the press conference was at HQ at eleven. With less than a half hour to get there, Jocelyn double-timed it through the crowded streets to the police station. Stepping through the security checkpoint, she headed to the conference room, where only a handful of reporters stood near the exit.

A spokesperson slid behind the lectern. "Good morning. I'm Gail Baskerville with Richmond Police. Thanks for coming. I have a brief statement about some recent crimes. I'll take questions at the end." Pausing to scan the mostly empty room, she continued, "Early this morning, there was a break-in at Jim's Gems on East Broad Street. The perpetrators drove a car through the front window around one and made off with a cache of jewelry. We're asking anyone with information to call Metro Richmond Crime Stoppers at 780-1000. Officers also recovered an unidentified male from the canal between Tredegar and the Fifth Street bridge. The male was pronounced dead at the scene. He is about five-foot-nine and one hundred eighty pounds. He has reddish-blond hair, looks to be between twenty-five and thirty-five, and was wearing a tuxedo. Anyone with information on his identity, please call Crime Stoppers. Questions?"

"Any camera footage on the jewelry store robbery?" a lanky reporter asked from the back of the room.

"The investigation's ongoing. We should have an update later today," Gail said.

Well, that was pretty much a bust. Jocelyn slipped out and hurried back to her office. *It's time for another tactic.*

At her desk, she pulled up Google Maps. There were no businesses near where the body was recovered. After a call to a nearby museum didn't yield any camera footage, she dialed Karl again.

"What, Josie?" he asked by way of a greeting.

"Karl, you know I love you. Are there any city cameras with footage down at the canal where the John Doe was found?"

"Kinda busy with the jewelry heist and a hit-and-run on Main Street. The floater's third on the list." He let out a long puff of air.

"I promise to bring treats the next time I see you," she said in her sweetest voice.

"Fine. One camera was damaged, so no feed. One picked up the victim walking toward the footbridge. Another shot showed him talking to a girl and then a few minutes later to one of the homeless guys in a wacky outfit. That's all I got. I like the chocolate eclairs from Fat Rabbit."

"Gotcha, and you're the best." Jocelyn disconnected.

After hours of searching Facebook groups, she almost blew past something. Someone had tagged a location on the canal with pictures of a wedding party. *Right date*, she thought. *And that explains the tux. It's my lucky day.* She scrolled, stopped, and sat back. "There you are," she said aloud, "and now I know your name."

"Whose name?" Dane Ervine, an overbearing reporter Jocelyn secretly called Boomer, asked. The stocky man with salt-and-pepper hair sat in the cube next to her.

"The guy RPD found floating in the canal this morning. I'm doing a follow-up for Eric. What are you working on?"

"New exhibit at the art museum and an arson/double homicide in Henrico. All in a day's work."

When he opened his laptop, stopping the conversation, Jocelyn returned to her search. Armed with the name she'd matched to the man in the water—Cam Lewis—she found only an outdated Facebook account. Although she wished she had more, she fired off an email to Karl with the picture of the wedding party. Then she scooped up her things and dropped them in her bag.

"Where are you off to?" Dane asked.

"Gotta run. Got people to talk to and stories to write." She gave a little wave and zipped out the door.

Planning her strategy in the elevator, she decided to do some good ol' gumshoe work to see if she could find anyone who'd seen the wedding party. When the elevator finally bumped down in the lobby, she changed her plan and made a beeline to the overstuffed orange sofas, where she spent twenty minutes messaging everyone tagged in the pictures with Cam.

To kill time while she waited for any replies, Jocelyn bought a sandwich and a canned drink from a food truck and hiked back to the Canal Walk. She staked out a bench in the partial shade of a pin oak tree. Thumbing through her newsfeed, she saw pictures of an Eighties tribute band from a concert on Brown's Island last night. Googling terms that might be related, she landed on some pictures, full of a mix of college students and Gen Xers reliving their heydays. No sign of any of the wedding party in the photos.

A rustling sound caught her attention, and she spotted J.P. rummaging through trash cans for recyclables. Tossing her lunch remains in the nearest receptacle, she emptied her Sprite can and walked toward the tall man, who wore a purple T-shirt, lime-green boa, and rainbow Converse tennis shoes.

"Hey, J.P.," she said. Not looking at her, he pulled a windshield wiper out of the trash and added it to the contents in his wagon. "It's me. Jocelyn. Do you want this for your collection?" She held out the can.

"Thanks, writer lady," he said, tossing it into the wagon.

"Were you out here last night?" she asked, as he continued to burrow in the trash can.

"Yeah. Great show, and lots of people left treasures behind," he said, not facing her. "I found some fancy women's shoes, a dress, and a bicycle tire near the bathrooms."

"Did you happen to see this group?" Jocelyn held up her phone.

The man, who reminded her of Hagrid in a feathered boa, lifted his head to squint at her phone. He blanched and took a step back. "Nope. I had nothing to do with him." He reached for the handle of his wagon. "But that's like the dress I found and the shoes. Weird."

When he moved on to the next trash can, Jocelyn followed. "I was hoping you could help me. I'm trying to find this man. The red-headed one."

"He's already been found," J.P. said. "I had nothing to do with it."

She cocked her head to one shoulder. "J.P., did you see him last night? Maybe before he ended up in the canal?"

"I couldn't help. I tried, but I couldn't," he muttered, shaking his head. "I really tried."

"Where did you see him?"

"He was sitting over there against the fence. I asked him if he was okay, but he didn't answer. I think someone took his wallet and phone."

"How could you tell?"

"His pockets were turned out, like Charlie Chaplin in the old movies. Or was it the Marx Brothers? I dunno."

"Was there anyone else around?"

"Nope. I figured he was sleeping. I went on with my work. He seemed okay. I didn't take nothing," he said and returned to his hunting.

"Thank you, J.P."

He waved one arm without pulling his head out of the can.

J.P. saw Cam alive. Could it have been an accidental death? There are a few places where there's no fencing. If Cam were drunk, he could have toppled in.

Deciding to head home to work on her story, Jocelyn wended her way through the side streets and an alley to her apartment building. She grabbed a tea from the almost-empty fridge and had just sat at her kitchen table when she got an alert. Nancy Highsmith had replied to her message. From her profile photo, Jocelyn recognized her as the tall blonde with a Seventies perm beside Cam in the wedding photo.

Jocelyn replied, *I'm sorry for your loss. Would you be able to talk to me today? I'm writing a story on Cam.*

How about Sacred Grounds near Monroe Park for coffee?

Is two o'clock good? Jocelyn typed.

Nancy replied with a thumbs-up emoji.

A little before two, Jocelyn found parking. Not seeing Nancy in the coffee shop full of artwork and brightly colored furniture, she ordered a vanilla latte and found a table facing the door.

A few minutes later, a curly-headed twentysomething in cargo pants, an olive jacket, and combat boots lumbered in and glanced around. "Are you Jocelyn?" she asked, standing behind a purple chair.

"Hi, Nancy. It's nice to meet you."

"Let me get something to eat. Be right back."

By the time she returned with a pimento cheese sandwich and a steaming mug of coffee, Jocelyn had perused her Facebook page.

"Thanks for seeing me at this sad time. Could you tell me a little about Cam?"

After swallowing her first bite of the sandwich, Nancy said, "We've been friends since college. We met at orientation, where we found out we had similar interests in comics and gaming. He works from home as an application developer for an insurance company and runs an online gaming guild in his spare time."

"I saw some of the wedding pictures. It looked like y'all were having fun."

"Yeah, I guess. Julie and Jamie Ellis got married on the roof of the Quirk Hotel. After the ceremony, we all decided to continue the party down at Brown's Island. Everyone seemed to have a good time. Well, maybe except for Cam."

Jocelyn leaned forward as Nancy took another bite of her sandwich. After a long pause and a gulp of her coffee, Nancy said, "He always had a thing for Julie, but nothing ever came of it."

"Did he like Jamie?"

"Roommates for four years. They were tight."

"So, no animosity about the wedding?"

"Not that he shared. We hung out a lot, playing games, but he wasn't really a talker."

"How did he act at the wedding?"

"Like the normal Cam. He was always super quiet, except when someone asked him about his new stuff, his new gaming furniture and bougie equipment. We teased him that he might never leave the house again."

"Was he drinking last night?"

"Yeah. We all were."

"Any issues at work or in his private life? Any enemies? Recent problems?"

A half-smile slid across Nancy's lips. "Nah. Cam went out of his way to avoid conflict. He had a good job that he liked. He made beaucoup bucks and enjoyed his toys. You know, the latest and greatest of everything. He acted like he was entitled to the very best."

The young woman's tone made Jocelyn look up from her notes before she asked when the girl had last seen her friend.

"I'm not sure. We took some photos down at the canal. Some of the gang were ready to leave, and others wanted to go to the concert."

"Which camp was Cam in?"

"Concert, I think. I went over to the margarita trucks, and I lost track of him after that. I hung out until about eleven, and then I headed home to get out of that itchy dress and awful shoes."

"No more contact with Cam after that?"

"No, sadly. I texted him a couple of times to see if he wanted to play, but I didn't get any response. I guess now I know why." Nancy sniffed and wiped her eyes. "That's all I know. We went through a lot together."

"Like what?"

"The crap that goes along with college and first jobs. And losing jobs."

"He lost a job?"

"No, I did. Two, in fact. It's hard to make enough to live on, and student loans bite." She waved her hand dismissively and clamped her lips shut.

"Thanks for talking with me. I know it's a difficult time. If you think of anything else, call me." Jocelyn slid her business card across the table. Nancy glanced at it and slipped it into one of the pockets of her cargo pants.

"I'm going to file a story on Cam this afternoon. Is there anything else you want folks to know about him?" Jocelyn asked.

"We're all hoping this was a horrible accident and that someone didn't do this to him on purpose."

"Anything else?" Jocelyn asked.

"Uh, do you know who I can talk to about his case? Like about next steps?"

"You can reach out to Richmond PD. They're in touch with his family."

"Oh, right. I guess they'd take care of his stuff." Nancy looked at her hands and rubbed several scratches.

Leaving the coffee shop, Jocelyn rushed to her car and dialed Karl.

"You know I have a day job," he said.

"I do. And you're so good at it," Jocelyn said in her syrupiest voice.

"Detective Hamlin said to tell you thanks for the help with the identification. Got any more tidbits for us?"

"I talked to one of his friends. Nancy Highsmith. She seemed a bit off. Maybe it's shock. Any chance the death was accidental?"

"Nope. Looks like robbery and assault. We got the homeless man near him on camera and another clip of someone in a hoodie walking with him around one o'clock near the canal."

"What was taken?"

"Hold your horses. I'm getting to that. Just refer to me as your anonymous source." After she agreed, he continued. "He had no phone, keys, or wallet on him. And when the super let the detective into his apartment, stuff was missing—like a giant screen TV and high-end gaming equipment. The super helped set it all up when it was delivered, so he knew about the gear."

"Okay, so Cam ends up face down in the canal after a friend's wedding, his wallet gone, and not twenty-four hours later, his expensive gadgets are stolen."

"Including two laptops."

"Hmmm." Jocelyn tapped her lips with her index finger.

"We're bringing in the homeless guy. Hopefully, we'll be able to wrap this up soon. I gotta run."

"Thanks, Karl," she said, thoughts turning to J.P. She didn't know him that well but couldn't see him pushing someone into the canal.

An Instant Messenger alert from Jesse Burns distracted her from her thoughts. *You wanted to talk to me about Cam? I'm still reeling.*

Sorry about your loss, she replied. *How did you know him?*

I'm in his guild.

Was he having trouble with anyone?

Yeah, someone was griefing him really bad. It totally freaked him out.

Jocelyn paused and did a quick search for gaming terms. "Griefing," she learned, meant "intentionally harassing another player."

Do you know who or why?

He didn't say. It all started after he got his sweet new gear.

If you remember anything else about it, reach out.

Sure.

The little flashing dots that indicated someone was typing disappeared.

Jocelyn headed home to finish her story, her thoughts going back to J.P. *He scavenges for things. He doesn't burgle apartments.*

The next day, Jocelyn busied herself with two other stories, but Cam and J.P. kept elbowing their way to the forefront of her thoughts. *It doesn't make sense that J.P. would kill Cam. There has to be more to the story. What did J.P. say about the clothes he found? And why would a bridesmaid dump her outfit in the trash near the canal walk?*

Looking up Nancy's address online, she decided to swing by after work for a few more questions.

About five-thirty, Jocelyn found parking on a side street and darted around the front of Nancy's building. When the elevator never arrived, she hoofed it up three flights of stairs and located apartment 312, but she had to thread her way around a bicycle, a red hand truck, a canvas wagon, and a stack of boxes. She banged on the door with one fist while taking a second look at all the stuff blocking the hall.

Shuffling sounds got louder behind the door, and Jocelyn banged again. "Nancy, it's Jocelyn."

The tall woman yanked the door open, her face half-hidden by her dark hoodie. "What? Oh, hi. I couldn't hear with my headphones on."

Behind the young woman, Jocelyn spotted more empty boxes and a ginormous television in front of a massive gamer's chair with cup holders and a footrest. A ratty loveseat and chair were pushed against a nearby wall.

"Nice digs you got here." Holding her camera at her waist, she snapped several photos, hoping they would show the contents of Nancy's living room. "My editor wants a follow-up story, and I thought I'd check in with you first. Can I come in?"

"Not much more to say," she said, moving to block Jocelyn's view of the apartment. "Sorry. I can't help you. Gotta get back to the tournament."

"Sure. Call me if you think of anything," Jocelyn said. "And hey, I was going to ask to see your bridesmaid's dress—"

Nancy slammed the door. Taking one last look at the clutter in the hallway, Jocelyn snapped a few more pictures. A half-torn label caught her eye. Cam Lewis. Heart beating faster, Jocelyn punched in Karl's number.

"You still working?" he asked, his voice gruff with exhaustion.

"I could say the same thing about you. Hey, I came over to Cam's friend's apartment to ask a few more questions, and something's not right here."

"Maybe not, but we have J.P. in custody. No sign of the vic's belongings, but we figure he's hocked all the computer stuff by now. He either pushed the guy in the canal, or he stumbled there on his own."

Jocelyn counted the empty boxes in the hall. "J.P. didn't take Cam's stuff."

"You sound like him. He's been pretty adamant that he didn't steal anything from the dead guy, but we'll see," Karl said.

A flash of movement behind Jocelyn made her whirl around.

"I think you need to mind your own business," Nancy hissed, brandishing a heavy wrench. She raised her arm to swing, and Jocelyn shoved the bicycle into the woman, knocking her off balance. Nancy's swing went wild, connecting with Jocelyn's wrist and making her drop her phone.

White stars flashed in front of Jocelyn's eyes. She tried to shake off the pain as Nancy climbed over the junk and scrambled toward her. When Nancy raised her arm again, Jocelyn gritted her teeth and sprang forward with the best banshee scream she could muster.

Nancy tripped over the wagon, the wrench clattering to the floor. Jocelyn lunged for the weapon, reaching it seconds before Nancy pounced. Rolling down the hallway, Jocelyn landed a solid kick to the other woman's middle. Nancy folded, clutching her ribs.

Ignoring her throbbing wrist, Jocelyn grasped the wrench with both hands and hit Nancy on the back of her head. A red stream slowly spread across her neck and trickled on the floor.

Jocelyn caught her breath and fished around for her phone. When she picked it up, she heard a tinny voice, "Jocelyn. Jocelyn, say something."

"Hi, Karl. I can't believe you're still on the line. Nancy attacked me, but I let her have it."

"I wouldn't expect anything less. Police are on their way. I'm sending an ambulance, too. You gave an old guy a heart attack. You okay?"

"I think she broke my wrist, but I'll live. Tell them to hurry. She's bleeding a lot."

"Will do. Hang in there."

Jocelyn leaned against the wall to wait, never taking her eyes off the woman on the floor. Nancy had killed her friend for gaming equipment, but there would be no more tournaments for the young woman now.

Game over, Nancy, she thought. *No rematch.*

A Sum of Parts

By May G. Kennedy

My name is Sidney Stone. Three months ago, when I retired from IT consulting, I moved to the tourist strip at Virginia Beach. It felt premature to move into an independent living community, but I couldn't resist an affordable apartment in an over-sixty facility with a view of an old wooden fishing pier. The pier juts out five hundred yards into the ocean and is still in constant use, so there's always something interesting to watch.

On a sunny afternoon two weeks after I bought the unit, I noticed that the pier had been cleared and yellow-taped off. I decided to stroll over to ask the displaced fishermen what had happened. As usual, my building's wheelchair-friendly elevator doors were painfully slow to open. Still a bit leery of the "community" aspect of my new living arrangement, I avoided eye contact as I passed residents peering through our ground-floor windows at the unusual activity on the beach.

When I reached the pier, I approached a stocky middle-aged woman who was holding a fishing rod and a battered plastic bucket.

"Catch anything?" I asked her.

"Nope, but those guys"—she swung her pail in their direction—"caught some five-pound bluefish."

"When was that?"

"Around four—right before we heard all the screaming."

"Screaming? What was that about?"

"Somebody reeled in part of a human arm! The Bicycle Beach Patrol guys showed up right away and cleared everyone off, and the EMTs just got here."

I looked up to see two emergency medical technicians carrying a large white ice chest down the huge old wooden structure. They loaded the cooler—now presumably arm-filled—into a waiting ambulance, which flashed its lights, emitted a single *whoop-whoop*, and pulled slowly onto Atlantic Avenue.

Imagining various horrible ways to lose an arm, I turned toward home. It was nearly time for April Lincoln, the facility's activities director, to drop by for a glass of wine. We met when she briefed me on my activity options as a new resident, and I'm happy to say that we've gotten together several times since then.

When she arrived, April asked, "Have you heard about the arm? It's all over the web, and some of the residents are pretty freaked out."

"Yes. In fact, I saw the EMTs cart it away."

She perched on the edge of my couch and poured herself a glass of wine. "Well," she informed me, "the breaking news is that it's a man's forearm, and there's a tattoo of the sun on the inside of his wrist."

"I'm surprised the police released that information so soon," I commented. "Maybe someone on the pier had already posted a cell phone picture, so holding it back would have been pointless. The tattoo should help identify the victim, but it won't help the cops figure out what happened to him, and—"

"I have an idea," she interrupted. "What if we organize a group of residents to follow the story and maybe even help the police, like amateur sleuths do on TV? Someone in the building might have known the dead person. And the arm was discovered in our backyard, practically, which should motivate the residents—well, the sharper ones—to get together and talk about it."

I made an ambiguous *umm* sound. My online stock-trading hobby requires a lot of focus, and I wasn't sure about letting April drag me into her latest project.

We switched on the local news to catch the severed-arm coverage, which was melodramatic but brief. April declined a second glass of wine, gave me a friendly pat on the shoulder, and left.

By morning, April had posted flyers announcing a discussion of the incident at the pier, and two people joined us at one that afternoon. One was a stocky black lady with a cane, who introduced herself as Etta Johnson—which was easy to remember, because Etta James, the great blues and jazz singer, grew up nearby. The other was young Sam Stokely, our maintenance guy. He seemed agitated and spoke first.

"I think I might know who lost that arm," he said. "There's a T-shirt shop called the Dirty Sinker a few blocks down Atlantic Avenue, and the owner has a sun tattoo on his wrist. The place is like always open, but it's been closed for the last couple of days."

"What else do you know about the owner?" Etta asked.

"I don't know his name," the custodian replied, "but he's like forty, and he's always trying something new to attract tourists. Nothing seems to work, though."

April opened her laptop and Googled the T-shirt shop. She found that it was owned by a Fred Fryer, and she entered this information into a citizen tip box on the police website. We agreed that our time had been well spent, exchanged phone numbers, and planned to reconvene the next day.

As we rose to leave, Etta asked me if I had time for a quick visit to the T-shirt shop. Unable to come up with a good excuse and somewhat curious myself, I agreed to take the field trip.

To make the outing easier for her—and, frankly, for me, too, given my tricky knee—I checked out a golf cart, and we rolled onto the bike path that runs parallel to the boardwalk. Soon after the cart's electric whine reached full pitch, it became clear that the victim of the crime (or accident) had already been identified. Through a gap in the beachfront hotel phalanx, we could see police at the T-shirt shop, and as we drew closer to the Sinker, we could see gloved personnel dusting and bagging.

"I doubt that whatever happened to Fred Fryer took place at his store," Etta opined.

"I agree. The shop has a security fence instead of a front wall, and the space isn't deep, so it's easy to see inside. Tourist season's over, but there are still people on the street. I bet the police would have gotten a 911 call if something violent happened there."

"Let's duck into that bar next door and ask a few questions," Etta proposed.

Nauti Nettie's was dark and musty and full of fish-themed kitsch art. We were the only customers. We sat at the bar, ordered beers, and asked the young bartender if she had known the T-shirt shop's owner.

"Sure, Fred comes in almost every night after he closes up shop. He loves our crab cakes. Oh, and he's a member of the Stock Dogs. That's an investment club that meets here every month. His arm is all we've been talking about today."

"How big is the club?" I asked.

"It has about twenty members, but only six or eight Dogs attend every meeting. Fred's one of the regulars. Of course, the club president always comes, too."

"And who's that?" Etta asked.

"Millicent Daltry."

"Is there anything else you can tell us about Fred?" Etta probed.

"Well, as I told the police, he's been having ex-wife problems."

"Oh, honey, do tell!" urged Etta.

The bartender leaned across the bar and lowered her voice. "It's no secret Fred's behind on his alimony. Francie was in here last week, complaining about it. By the time Fred showed up for dinner, she was drunk, and she threw a drink at him. I had to ask her to leave and, on her way out, she yelled that she'd get what he owed her—one way or another."

We overtipped and stepped outside into a misting rain. Once snugly under the golf cart's canopy, we Googled the Stock Dogs' president on my phone and learned that Millicent Daltry managed a local beauty salon that catered to African Americans.

"Any interest in a manicure?" I asked Etta.

At our "arm mystery" meeting the following day, I began to report what we'd learned at Nauti Nettie's, but Etta interjected, "I went to Millicent Daltry's beauty salon last night and got a manicure and some *scoop!*"

According to the salon owner, the Stock Dogs club had been founded in the late Nineties, when interest in learning about the market was spurred by the dramatic early success of the dot-com start-ups. Monthly contributions were just twenty dollars per member. Most of the members had gone to high school together in Virginia Beach, so the club was mainly a way to keep in touch. In my experience, the stock market *can* make socializing a lot easier.

The investment club had survived two market busts. Millicent's monthly loss/gain reports now showed a respectable rate of return, and no one had ever left the group officially. But meeting attendance had waned over the years. Millicent had heard that Fred Fryer's T-shirt shop was struggling, and she was also aware of his alimony debt, so she wasn't surprised when he announced six weeks ago that he wanted to cash out.

"I wonder if cashing him out caused any problems for the club," mused April.

"It did!" Etta responded. "According to Millicent, Dave Barrymore—the accountant who keeps the club's books—had to figure out how to calculate an individual member's share. It was taking time, and Fred was getting impatient."

Etta smiled triumphantly. She sat back in her chair, gracefully crossing one hand over the other so we could admire her bright turquoise fingertips.

My phone chimed a news update, and I read aloud: "A preliminary medical exam indicated that the victim's forearm was reeled in from the fishing pier within twenty-four hours of his death. It was severed from the body of the deceased postmortem. Wounds were consistent with a shoulder bite from a large marine predator. A formal coroner's report is pending, but without recovering the body, establishing a definitive cause of death is unlikely."

Custodian Sam leaned back and speculated, "I'll bet Francie Fryer lured Fred out on a boat and then like shot him or stabbed him and pushed him overboard. Then a great white shark went after the juicy trunk meat—pardon the gory details—and the current carried Fred's forearm to the pier. Meanwhile, whatever's left of him will be dinner for scavenging critters for a week."

Etta continued, "I wonder if he had any life insurance to garnish for back alimony. Or maybe Francie could sell the stuff in his shop."

"I'd like to know how much money Fred would have gotten from the stock-club cashout," April added. "You know a lot about stocks, Sidney. Maybe we could meet with the Stock Dogs' accountant and tell him that…that we want to start an investment club here in the building. It shouldn't be hard to work the conversation around to how successful his original club was. And who knows," she chirped, "we might *really* start an investment club!"

I shrugged noncommittally, daunted by the prospect of mentoring co-investors with fixed incomes and waning powers of recall. Still, I wasn't going to turn down an outing with April.

I Googled "Dave Barrymore accountant Virginia Beach" and found a skimpy website containing his photo, an office address, and a phone number. I left a recorded message that Ms. Lincoln and I would come to his office that afternoon.

Barrymore's "office" turned out to be a rented cubicle in a dying suburban mall. Our footsteps echoed as we walked from the empty food court to the wing that housed the office spaces.

At first, it seemed strange that the glass door to the cube pod was unlocked, but we soon saw that there was nothing there to steal. We communicated by exaggerated pantomime as we searched for the space number listed on the accountant's website.

"Don't touch anything," April whispered.

"There aren't any signs saying 'Keep Out' or 'Official Crime Scene,' so I guess it's okay to be here," I answered softly. "But you have a point." I pulled out my trusty blue bandana and draped it over my hand.

The single file drawer in Dave Barrymore's battered metal desk contained two thin folders.

"There's nothing here but some take-out menus and Bitcoin propaganda, and it's too dark to read. April, shine your phone flashlight on these papers, and I'll take pictures of them. Then we can put everything back the way it was and look at the photos later."

I shot the fronts and backs of the half-dozen sheets of paper and restored them to their folders. As we emerged from the office space into the mall, I noticed security cameras and tried not to look suspicious.

April knew a family-owned wood-paneled seafood-and-steak restaurant on nearby Thalia Creek called Steinhilber's. It has thrived since 1939 by serving fried shellfish and shrimp, balanced by chilled iceberg lettuce wedges topped with blue cheese crumbles. The old standby eatery still earns high ratings on Tripadvisor, and it sounded good to me.

We were seated right away. The substantial heft of the restaurant's damask napkins and scuffed monogrammed cutlery made me sigh with nostalgia. A waitress brought sweating glasses of ice water and lemon halves crowned with little hairnets to catch the seeds. We sipped classic cocktails, while I scrolled through the photos of the file papers and tried not to grin like a fool when April shifted closer to see my phone screen.

Most of the menus in Dave Barrymore's file were from fast-food joints some distance from the ocean, signaling meager finances or a local's lack of interest in the beach or both. The Bitcoin literature just described the cryptocurrency, but April detected a shadow on the back of one sheet. I complimented her powers of observation and promised to conduct a full photo-forensic analysis when I got back to my big computer screen at the condo. She flashed me a self-satisfied smile, and then the oyster appetizer arrived, demanding our full attention.

By the next morning, I had used photo-editing software to sharpen the image of the shadow, which turned out to be grooves in the paper left by someone writing on a covering sheet. I could make out "AA 2990" and guessed that was an American Airlines flight number. Sure enough, a non-stop from nearby Norfolk International to Miami with that flight number was scheduled to depart at six-thirty that evening.

I emailed my findings to the other three members of our investigative foursome and leaned back in my ergonomic chair to watch dolphins arch out of the surf.

Etta phoned me within minutes. "Francie Fryer had the most obvious motive, but we need to take a hard look at that accountant right now! If you add up his dispute with Fred Fryer, his empty office space, and the flight number on that paper, I bet that that sorry number-cruncher had something to do with Fred's death and is making a break for it! Once he gets to Miami, leaving the country should be easy, and he could get away with murder!"

I had to admit that the need for action was urgent. I called April, and she agreed to give the information we'd gathered to a policewoman she knew on the local force. "She gives self-defense and anti-fraud lectures to our residents every year. We work together very well. I'm sure she'll pass our leads on to the right person."

A half-hour later, April phoned me back. Her contact had disclosed that accidental drowning hadn't been ruled out in the Fryer case, and the police had interviewed the angry ex-wife twice. Francie had vehemently and colorfully denied any involvement in Fred's disappearance, but she lived alone and didn't have an alibi for the estimated time of death. The officer had pulled reservations for the Miami flight, but Dave Barrymore's name wasn't on the list.

My teeth clenched in frustration. Barrymore could simply buy a last-minute plane ticket at the airport and get away with Fred's murder. I found his home address in the online white pages and texted young Sam to request a ride to the accountant's house.

Sam's pick-up truck soon appeared in the loading zone in front of our building, and I climbed in as fast as my knee would allow. We sped to Barrymore's address and cautiously approached the house on foot.

The modest asphalt-shingled structure occupied a corner lot. There were no lights on inside. A short driveway led from the street to a windowless garage behind the house.

"Let's see if there's a car in there," Sam suggested. He sneaked up to the garage's side door, found it locked, and pulled a screwdriver out of his pocket. Before I knew it, we had access. I realized that I was growing a bit suspicious of Sam. After all, he had taken a surprising interest in meeting with a group of oldsters, he had identified the victim, and now he was demonstrating skill at breaking and entering….

Shaking off my doubts, I followed him into the garage. We were greeted by a sharp bleach smell and, as our eyes adjusted to the gloom, a motorboat on a wheeled trailer took shape. Inside the boat, we saw a heavy anchor chain but no anchor.

The sound of a car crunching onto the graveled driveway startled us, and we crouched down—me behind the boat and Sam behind a big bag of mulch. We held our breath as the car door slammed, and someone walked past the garage and into the house through its back door.

Several minutes passed before Barrymore turned on a television, and we dared to move. I took quick pictures of the boat and the anchorless anchor chain, and we crept out of the garage and past the accountant's old Buick. When we reached Sam's truck, I needed a minute to calm down.

"I'll bet it went down like this," Sam said. "Fred gets tired of waiting for his Stock Dogs money, and he goes to Dave Barrymore's home to, like, demand his cash-out. Things get hot, and Fred somehow gets killed. Barrymore takes the body out to sea, weighs it down with his anchor, and dumps it overboard. When he gets back home, he douses his boat deck with bleach to destroy any blood and DNA evidence."

I picked up the thread. "I'd guess that nobody but Barrymore has looked at the club's actual bank statements for years: he just sent Millicent a monthly email with the current stock value and the amount of cash on hand for investment. He was planning to make off with the money eventually, and once Fred's arm got reeled in, he kicked his exit plan into high gear!"

At the sound of a car, we turned and saw Dave's old Buick back out of his driveway and round the corner. "He's heading for the airport!" I exclaimed.

Sam consulted his watch and growled, "The damn flight to Miami leaves in an hour!"

We took off in pursuit of the Buick, and I called April to explain what we thought was happening. I sent her the boat pictures, and she agreed to forward them to her police contact and to grab Etta and meet us at the airport as soon as possible.

We lost Barrymore en route, and I worried that we'd be too late to block his escape. But soon after the women joined us in the Departures Hall, Etta recognized him from his website picture.

April reported the sighting to her police contact, and we waited with growing distress as our suspect breezed through security and hustled out of sight. Just after the final boarding call for the Miami flight, though, two TSA officials walked our perp back through the checkpoint and into the custody of a pair of uniformed police officers. We were thrilled and quite proud of ourselves.

The following morning, April's contact on the police force met with us to bring us up to date. As we sipped decaf and nibbled elegant cookies, the officer thanked us for our help and reported that Dave Barrymore had confessed to killing Fred Fryer by accident during a struggle, anchoring the body, and dumping it at sea. The accountant had been charged with embezzlement and second-degree murder and was being held without bail.

It appeared that the crime had occurred almost exactly as Sam and I had surmised. Barrymore used a fake passport at the airport, and a thumb drive found in his carry-on luggage contained personal key codes worth about two million dollars in Bitcoin, which would be returned to the Stock Dogs and other clients he'd defrauded.

Our little group is without a mystery to solve at present, but anything can happen at any time in a freewheeling tourist town like Virginia Beach, so we stay in touch. Etta and I play bridge once a week. April found a classic film series at Old Dominion University in nearby Norfolk, and we attend together. Sam's still our custodian, but he's applied to the police academy. I recall my suspicions of him with some chagrin.

And, yes, I gave in to April's suggestion that we start an investment club at our facility—on the condition that I maintain its financial records myself. I wasn't just humoring her. The Case of the Severed Arm showed me that some of my neighbors still have their wits about them, so we could very well make each other some money! I'm starting to see that, when one resident loses an ability to the passing years, someone down the hall can probably compensate.

And I can live with that.

From Here to Serenity

By Kristin Kisska

Rita

When the front doorbell jingles, I stand behind my desk. A tall, athletic man enters the small office space. His presence fills the doorway, absorbing all the oxygen in the room. He feels larger than life in person. I've only seen photos until now.

After glancing around the reception area from behind his sunglasses, the man reads the front of the envelope he's holding. "Is this the Serenity Salon?"

My massage parlor is located on a quiet side street in Richmond's festive Carytown but on a block without any restaurants or boutiques, so it's not as well known. Perfect for my purposes.

"Yes, you've found the right place. Welcome." I do my best to keep a steady voice despite my heart jackhammering in my chest. "And you are?"

"Beagle. Jonathan Beagle." He looks as awkward as a nun at a rave. "My wife gave me a gift certificate for a hot-stone massage."

"Of course, Mr. Beagle. I've been expecting you." He's a few minutes late for his appointment but doesn't apologize. I'm relieved he showed. "May I see your driver's license?"

He fishes his wallet from his pocket and turns a full circle, inspecting the reception area. I try to envision the space through his lens. Personally, it gives a little too much generic-office vibe for my taste, but I'm proud of how well I spruced up my pop-up day spa. Gauzy fabric draped across the front window doubles as a privacy barrier. Two sage-green chairs flank the corner. A bouquet of white flowers graces the reception desk. A table lamp offers muted mood lighting. An antique mirror hangs behind the desk. Water trickles over a tiered rock arrangement on a coffee table. And diffused essential oils generate citrusy notes throughout.

I fake a cough, clear my throat, and motion to the surgical facemask I'm wearing. "I'm sure it's allergies, but I'd rather be safe than sorry."

This handsome man is about as far away from his comfort zone as he can get without leaving his ZIP code. He won't be uncomfortable for long. He slowly eyeballs my black scrubs from head to toe and shrugs, dismissing me. "Whatever."

I double-check his name and address, then hand back his ID, along with a clipboard. "Please fill out this paperwork."

"Seriously? I thought this was supposed to be relaxing."

"It will be. I promise. But I need to know of any surgeries, injuries, or health concerns before I start the massage."

"Just some broken bones, a dislocated shoulder, and an ACL repair." He scribbles notes on the paper but glances up to wink at me. "College football. First string."

Fighting my cringe, I force my body to relax. Two regular-season games into his junior year, he was booted from the team for doping. Lost his scholarship. Never graduated. Never lost the chip on his shoulder, either.

He doesn't know that I know.

"Follow me, please." We don't have far to go.

This commercial space is three rooms and a half bath. Bigger than I needed to rent, but the owner let me pay cash. As I open the door to the salon room, the hanger with the men's waffle-weave robe knocks against the wall. Dim lights from illuminated salt blocks and soft woodwind music punctuated with rhythmic crashing waves welcome us. My heated massage table looms front and center, covered in soft jersey sheets and a cream blanket.

Motioning to the chair in the corner, I give my standard instructions. "Take your time. Everything comes off but your boxers. When you're ready, lie on the table face-up, under the blankets. I'll knock before entering."

"I can't go nude?"

My cough is real this time. "Not unless you want to be burned." I slip out of the room to compose myself.

While waiting for him to change, I lock the deadbolt on the front door and text a photo I'd stealth-snapped to Jenny.

Jenny

I arrive at JJ's morning preschool drop-off line, hoping to get in and out quickly. When it's our turn, my son hops out of the car and runs towards the entrance ahead of the teacher escorting him. Then, I steer around the curve to exit the school zone. But the preschool director motions me over to their parking lot.

Oh, no. I override my temptation to ignore her instructions and beeline to the exit. My stomach sinks as I put the car in park and lower my window. While she walks over, I check my face in the rearview mirror. I look like a freight train ran over me.

"Good morning, Mrs. Beagle." The director's expression is equal parts concern, professionalism, and kindness. I expect you need all three to work with a hundred preschoolers daily.

Mumbling a greeting, I angle my face to hide the bruises around my eye. I know what she wants to talk about, but I'm not up to the task of finessing.

"Last Friday, JJ punched and kicked one of his classmates. His teacher separated them before anyone got hurt, but her parents were understandably upset."

"I'm sorry. I'm sure JJ just forgot his manners." It's still impossible for me to envision my sweet four-year-old son hitting anyone. "You know how little boys are, all energy and fearlessness."

"Yesterday, when the teacher contacted Mr. Beagle about the situation, he—"

I draw a shaky breath. Oh, I know what happened next. That's the reason I'm wearing dark sunglasses on an overcast morning.

"—he yelled obscenities at her and threatened to smash her windshield with a baseball bat."

My pulse races. All I can do is stutter an apology on my husband's behalf. I don't know if my response is in any way intelligible. Something about how I'm sure he didn't mean it. Jonathan can see my phone location, and he'll ask why I stayed so long at the school.

"If JJ continues this aggressive behavior, we'll be forced to suspend him and perhaps take additional actions with the authorities. Both your son's and husband's behavior are alarming. We take *all* of our students' and teachers' well-being seriously." The director's voice is firm. Her message is clear.

I nod. What else can I do? I'm stuck. I'd hoped registering JJ in preschool would expose him to playtime, friends, and lessons, show him that a big, wide, friendly world awaits him. It's too late for me.

"Mrs. Beagle, I'm concerned." The director's brow furrows as she inspects my face. My injuries are bigger than usual this time, but JJ has already missed enough school, and I didn't think they'd ask to talk to me. "Are things safe for you and JJ at home?"

My breath hitches. I glance over my shoulder, but no one is close enough to overhear us. Did JJ tell his teacher something? They'll surely take him away from me, and I don't think I could survive without my son. A four-year-old boy needs his mama. We look out for each other. We need each other. If Jonathan finds out I've told anyone, we'd—I'd—

I can't let my mind go to that place. Too dark. Too real. My hands shake, drawing the director's notice, so I grip the steering wheel until my knuckles blanch. I focus on keeping my breathing steady.

"Email Rita," the director says. "I—I was in a similar situation a while ago. She helped me." She hands me a folded piece of paper and, with a sad smile, steps away from my car. "Please be safe."

The lump in my throat makes it hard to swallow. The preschool director is the only person in the last five years who's shown me a hint of concern. I've gotten so used to hiding and pretending that everything is normal that I'm not sure I can even process her kind gesture. I don't know who this Rita person is. Doctor? Police officer? Lawyer? Counselor? But help is something I desperately need.

As soon as I get home, I unfold the note. Handwritten on it is a long alphanumeric email address. Blinking back unshed tears, I stuff it deep inside my purse. Jonathan and I share an email address, which he monitors like a hawk. Contacting Rita will be tricky, but I have an idea.

The next day, JJ and I visit our library's morning storytime. I sneak out to the computer bank and create an anonymous email account. With shaking hands, it takes me four tries to type Rita's long email address correctly. My subject line has two words: *Please help.*

When I get the chance to return to the library, Rita had replied with a phone number and instructions. *Call from a burner phone.*

It takes another few days to figure out how to get cash, buy the phone, and find a quiet, safe place to make the call, all without Jonathan knowing. If he finds out, he'll kill me.

The first two times I dialed, I let it ring but then hung up before anyone could answer. What was I doing? I don't even know this person. Can I trust her?

But on the third try, I stay on the line.

"Rita?" I say, when someone picks up. "This is Jenny."

Rita

After gently knocking, I reenter the spa room. Jonathan lies face up on my warming massage table, with only his bare shoulders and head exposed. I dim the lights, insert a rolled towel under his knees. While adjusting the top sheet for better access to his limbs, I ask in my librarian tone, "Are you comfortable?"

He grunts his yes. A contented grin overtakes his face. "This is my first massage since my college football days. Our trainer used to work on my throwing arm after practices and games, but the locker room was never this nice. Damn, I miss those days."

"Indeed." Though I discourage conversation during deep-tissue massages with one-word answers, I can't stop my clients from spending the time as they wish. It no longer surprises me that people use their spa appointments to vent their troubles, like they would to a priest, therapist, or bartender.

I'm none of those.

Technically speaking, I'm not a massage therapist, either. I was certified as a medic many years ago. So much trauma. So much pain. I helped fix the aftermath of too many preventable atrocities. Then there were the ones who'd cried for help, but we arrived too late. They broke my heart and inspired me to change my career. To level the playing field. To intervene *before* the assault instead of repairing the victims afterward. To give the helpless a chance.

The path to serenity can present itself in so many forms. I'm just the medium to release the pains of life. My goal is to offer a sense of weightlessness from mind, body, and spirit through detoxing. After mixing essential oils—sweet orange, lavender, and rosewood—I rub the aromatherapy tincture on my hands and move to the head of the table.

"Breathe deeply. Three times." I hold my palms inches above his face as he inhales. Then I begin kneading his pecs and shoulders.

I never advertise. Word of my concierge services is shared discretely from those who have benefited to others in need. My own whisper network. No surprise, I receive far more requests than I can accommodate. That's why I vet my potential clients with a screening call. Over the past decade, I've come to be able to tell within the first ten seconds of the phone call if the client hits my sweet spot. I don't do revenge. Or anger. Or hopelessness. Or injustice.

No. I only help those women who are in mortal fear. Who are at the brink of hell and are in danger of being pushed over the edge. Who can't escape because of young children or circumstances. Who've avoided becoming a statistic on an actuarial chart thanks to their honed survival instincts.

The unlucky women that humanity and law enforcement forget.

Jonathan groans in relaxed appreciation as I work my way clockwise around the table. Though I try to tune out his drivel, he waxes on about his wife. How she got pregnant on the sly, roping him into a shotgun wedding.

"Say," he says, "I feel like I can relate to you. Your hands are incredible.

Think I can get your number?"

Charming.

It's all I can do to keep my massage pressure steady and not show anything but professional indifference while he claims how tolerant he's been.

Jenny's X-rays tell a different story.

She pinged my radar before I ever heard her voice. When she called me, she hung up the first two times. Then, her clipped words were punctuated with notes of terror, and her story only confirmed what I already believed at my primordial core. That extra sense that all females are born with, along with our extra X chromosome. We drew the short straw in the universe's lottery of privilege.

Jenny told me she lives in Richmond. I know the Old Dominion well. Though I host many screening calls from Virginians, I can't set up my pop-up spa in the same location too often, or I risk leaving a breadcrumb trail for investigators to follow. But it's been several years since my last client here.

Still, I can't be too careful. Thus, the long alphanumeric email address to protect my identity. Rita's not my real name, of course. I assumed it after discovering that St. Rita of Cascia was the patron saint of abuse victims.

Soft music continues to play as I finish rubbing Jonathan's right arm.

My fees are high. It's neither cheap nor easy living off-grid and one step ahead of the law. Normally, by this point in the massage, I would expect to have received a text confirmation from my bank that the balance of my fee had been paid.

If not—and sometimes this happens—my client has changed her mind, and she lets me know by not paying. That's okay, too. They only forfeit their deposit. When that happens, my hot-stone massage progresses in the standard way.

Every case I accept touches my soul, but Jenny's is particularly heart-wrenching. After all these years, hers was only the third case I've ever taken *pro bono*. Instead of a message from my bank, all I need is Jenny's text to proceed.

Jenny

How long has it been since I learned about Rita? Three weeks? A month?

When I called her on the burner phone, Rita didn't interrupt me once. The pause at the end made me wonder if she'd hung up on me halfway through my sad, twisted tale. But finally, she responded. "Do you love him?"

I didn't answer right away. I do—or at least I did—love Jonathan. Is it possible to love and hate someone with every fiber of your being? If so, that's where I am. Clinging to survival day by day—hour by painful hour, by the grace of God. He gets so uncontrollably angry. It's no longer a question of *if* Jonathan will eventually kill me but *when*. Today a fist, tomorrow a tire iron.

Dread coils in the pit of my stomach. What will happen to JJ when I'm gone and can't protect him? Not for the first time, I see my son as a miniature towheaded version of his father.

My hesitancy revealed everything Rita needed to know. But when she told me her fee, my lungs collapsed. My freedom closed in on me like a vise. She might as well have asked for a gazillion dollars. Rita's fee was exorbitant, but she worked with me.

A few weeks later, here I am. JJ is sitting on my lap, and with a dozen other moms and preschoolers we listen to the librarian read a stack of picture books at our weekly storytime.

My alibi.

Rita's text hit my burner phone ten minutes ago. She sent a photo of the preestablished body part: a sketched football goalpost with a large 21 in the middle, his jersey number. It's him. His tattoo. On his neck. Jonathan is with her at the spa right now.

Honestly, I never thought he would fall for the bait. A hot-stone massage? When Rita first suggested the idea, I almost hung up on her. But he loved it. Apparently, his football trainer used to knead his muscles all the time in college, before he lost his scholarship and dropped out of school.

I met him right after. He was nicer, then. He would munch on the Endless Fries platter at my diner's counter and flirt with me until I clocked off my shift. Before I knew it, I was pregnant with JJ, married by a justice of the peace, and we'd moved away from all my friends to Richmond for his job. His first punch sent me into preterm labor. It only got worse from there.

I stare at the phone.

These past few weeks, I've prayed that there was a different answer. My bruises and cuts and broken bones healed, so perhaps my husband's nature would do the same. Gifting him the hot-stone massage actually seemed to be the miracle I was hoping for. He began to be nicer to us. More caring—dare I say gracious. He must've felt appreciated. I thought that I'd resurrected the old Jonathan. The one who treated me as a prize to be won. Not trash to be burned.

Last night, though, Jonathan again turned his aggression on JJ. I had to order my son out of the house for his safety. He hid in the overgrown shrubs under his bedroom window, shivering in the cold, until I hobbled outside to get him.

How many times can a woman be a human shield?

Turns out the answer is infinite times, at least when it comes to protecting my son.

My adorable JJ sits on my lap, enchanted by the story the librarian is reading. I inhale the freshly bathed scent of his soft, baby-fine hair. He would never turn into his father, right? Not my sweet-natured son. He's so loving with me. He deserves better than Jonathan. Both of us do.

We can't keep living like this. My heart aches for the childhood he's experiencing. No child should have to hide from his own father.

Rita is our last hope. She's waiting for my reply—my final acceptance of our fate. Our future.

For me? No. I don't care about me. I'm doing this for my son.

I pick up the burner phone. With an out-of-body sensation, I witness myself typing the code to proceed: *Thank you.*

Rita

Jenny's *Thank you* buzzes my phone as I'm inserting the head cradle at the top of my massage table. This moment never fails to stab me in my gut. The universe reminds me of why I'm doing what I do.

My older sister and my young nephew could've used a Rita. My brother-in-law was charged with their deaths. But legal justice was too little, too late. He gets to continue living behind bars. It won't bring them back from the beyond. My parents died brokenhearted.

I couldn't help my loved ones, but I can help others in similar situations. Like Jenny and her JJ. She reminds me of my sister, who met my brother-in-law while she, too, was waiting tables at a diner.

My day of reckoning will come. I'll be labeled a serial killer.

But until then, I can rescue a few more of the many women and children who fall through the cracks in our system, one hot-stone massage at a time.

When Jonathan turns over, I inch him up until he's lying face down with no view except the floor and my shoes. On a stool elevated close to his face, I place a steaming bowl of essential oils and ether vapors to help him relax. The face cradle's cushion against his jaw makes talking uncomfortable. Works for me. I'd rather hear the woodwinds and rhythmic waves of my spa music than his drivel.

After a few more minutes of massaging his neck and back, I collect the heated stones. With a soothing voice, I give a gentle warning. "I will lay six stones along your spine, one at a time. They are scalding hot, but the sting goes away within seconds. Then, I'll place a sheet over your back while you absorb the warmth. Are you ready?"

"Go for it." He's so relaxed at this point his words slur.

As I place the first stone at his waist, his back contracts, and he hisses. But just as quickly, he relaxes again. I do the same with the second stone, just a few inches up his spine. Then, the third.

Sometimes, I marvel at my ability to practice relaxation techniques on human monsters—the men who prey on the fairer sex. It would be so much faster to blow their brains out. But then I remember there's more than one path to serenity. I hope St. Rita approves. In my heart, I feel my sister's blessing.

By the time I place the fourth stone, he's used to the routine and no longer flinches at the heat. Perfect.

As I place the fifth stone, my extra-fine syringe pierces his flesh and is removed before the injection's sting—masked by the stone's heat—dissipates.

Followed by the final stone and the sheet. He's snoring as I set the alarm on my phone for thirty-five minutes. That's all the time I'll need to pack my pop-up spa's materials into my five bins.

When his snoring fades, I check his pulse and temperature. He's drifting. It won't be long now.

I pack the unmarked white van parked behind the building with my bins. Ten minutes to go. I scour all the knobs and switches on the empty office space with a bleach solution. Then I slide his body off the table to the floor, leaving his clothes and wallet by his side.

When my alarm vibrates, my trusty massage table is stowed in the van and temporarily retired—until our next client needs us.

I text Jenny: *Done.*

Sending serenity vibes to the universe, I pray for my sister to watch over her. I hope Jenny and JJ get the do-over they deserve. But I won't find out, unless their story makes the news. They will never hear from me again, and my phone will be destroyed before nightfall. I take a secondary highway to the North Carolina border. Somewhere along the way, when I can find a quiet exit, I'll ditch my wig and change the license plates on my van.

I've always liked Virginia, but I hope I don't need to return anytime soon. Not for work, at least. Maybe next time I'll visit on vacation.

Goodbye for now, Richmond.

The Perfect Job

By Josh Pachter

When I completed my master's at UVA, there weren't any full-time professor gigs advertised in my field in the 804, and because I had family in the area, I wasn't interested in moving elsewhere. So I became what is known as a "road scholar," teaching as much as I could at what was then still called John Tyler Community College at the Midlothian and Chester campuses and driving north on I-95 to Fredericksburg and west on I-64 to Charlottesville to add part-time work at several other schools in order to cobble together something approximating a full-time income.

One of my adjunct positions had me teaching at the men's prisons in Buckingham and Dillwyn for a program that partnered the Virginia Department of Corrections with Piedmont Virginia Community College, and the first of the two days I want to tell you about happened at Buckingham, where I was teaching a course in public speaking in the spring of 2018.

(What use do incarcerated felons have for public speaking? In fact, what use do incarcerated felons have for a college education in the *first* place? You may well ask. The thing is, it costs more than twenty thousand dollars a year to house a convict in the Old Dominion and less than *two* thousand a year to educate him…and the recidivism rate for cons released *with* a college education is about seventy percent lower than it is for those released *without*. That's why, once upon a time, Congress authorized Pell Grants to cover the tuition cost for inmates within five years of their parole dates—at least until a sufficient number of outraged parents who couldn't afford post-secondary schooling for their *own* kids objected loudly enough to seeing their tax dollars used to buy post-secondary schooling for the guys who'd burgled their houses badgered the House and Senate into cancelling the program. It's a shame the G caved, as the numbers really speak for themselves: education helps turn incarceration from a punishment and a revolving door into a rehabilitative experience that makes parolees significantly less likely to reoffend. Short-sighted, outraged parents! Short-sighted, Congress!)

Anyway, so I was teaching a morning class in public speaking at Bucky in 2018.

One of my first assignments in that course is a round of ungraded impromptu speeches. "Impromptu," if you don't speak the lingo, means "off the cuff," "ad lib," "off the top of your head," "without any prior preparation or rehearsal time."

The way it works is that I bring to class an envelope filled with little slips of paper, on each of which I have printed a topic for impromptu speaking. Simple stuff, like *The Best Meal I Ever Ate, What I'd Do If I Was Elected President, My Favorite Music*, like that.

I call the students one by one up to the front of the room. I fan out the strips of paper, printed side down, and have each person pick one. He flips it over and sees the topic, hands the slip back so I can reuse it with my next group, and then speaks impromptu for one to two minutes. When he's done, we all applaud his courage, and I give him a couple of pieces of praise (i.e., "You had direct eye contact with the audience, and you spoke loudly enough so that everyone can hear you") and a couple of suggestions (i.e., "I recommend you keep your hands out of your pockets and available for gesturing, and it would be a good idea not to punctuate your sentences with meaningless noises such as *like* and *um* and *y'know*"), and then we move on to the next speaker.

So on this day I'm telling you about, the third or fourth guy I called up to the front of the room was a man I'm going to call John, not generically like "John Doe," but because his first name actually happened to *be* John. He shambled up from his seat, and I fanned out my slips of paper for him to choose from.

Now, John was a *big* guy, and he was all muscle, the kind of guy if you saw him coming toward you in Shockoe Bottom after dark, you'd step out of his way, maybe even cross the street. He was bullet-headed and clean-shaven, and when he rolled up the sleeves of his orange jumpsuit there was ink on both of his forearms. The usual stuff—a tiger, an eagle, a Celtic knot—all quite tasteful. No prison tats or gang symbology.

He was doing time for a drug offense. Actually, most of my students were in for drug offenses. I never *asked* them what had brought them to prison, but they usually wanted to make sure I knew they weren't rapists or murderers or, worst of all, child molesters. (There *were* rapists and murderers and child molesters in the house, but they rarely attended college. Most of those guys were either doing a sentence without the possibility of parole and thus ineligible for the educational programs or else a lot more interested in working out on the Nautilus equipment and bulking up their bodies than in going to school and bulking up their brains.)

Anyway, back to John. I always take a look at the selected topic slip when the student returns it to me, so I know what it is he's *supposed* to be talking about, and John's slip read *The Perfect Job*.

I'm still teaching today, and I still use that as one of my topics. Over the years, I've probably heard *hundreds* of "perfect job" impromptus, and usually the student—whether it's a tough-guy incarcerated felon or an eighteen-year-old fresh-out-of-high-school kid who's going to community college because Mommy and Daddy told him (or her, or nowadays them) *either take some classes at the nearest CC or start paying rent on your bedroom*—will talk happily about the summer he spent selling ice cream out of a truck ting-a-linging its way through suburban neighborhoods or hopefully about a dreamt-of career as an NFL footballer or a successful rapper or movie star or model.

John, though, stood there at the front of the room, muscles bulging, and blithely told us about a robbery he'd pulled to support his MDMA habit, a robbery for which he had never been caught. A "perfect job," get it?

We all applauded the speech, I offered praise and suggestions for improvement, and class continued. When we finished for the day, I walked across the wide grassy yard that separated the building in which I held my sessions from the administration building through which I entered and exited the prison.

And before I cleared through security, I told a guard I had something to report.

See, one of the requirements for teaching at a correctional facility in the Commonwealth of Virginia is that I have to promise to pass along any evidence of felonious activity that comes to my attention … and big dumb John had just flat-out confessed to an unsolved robbery.

So I reported it, and—surprise!—John wasn't in class the following week, and he never showed up again for the rest of the semester. I was tempted to ask the other guys if they knew what had happened to him but finally decided that discretion was the better part of valor and avoided the subject.

Okay, so, if this was a movie, at this point, we'd zoom in to a close-up of a month-by-month calendar hanging on the wall, and pages would start dropping off to show the passage of time, and the audience would realize that three years have gone by.

Which brings us to the second of the two days I want to tell you about, early autumn 2021, three years later.

COVID had loosened its grip on higher ed by then, and I was back at Buckingham, this time teaching a night class, not in public speaking but in—of all things—film appreciation. (And how was *that* supposed to keep a parolee from reoffending? I have no idea. But film appreciation is one of my favorite courses to teach—I love seeing Twenty-First Century students discover that silent films, and black-and-white films, and even *musicals* might not be quite as stultifyingly boring as they'd assumed they were—so, when I am offered the opportunity, I grab it.)

On the night in question, we'd spent three hours talking about German Expressionism, and I'd shown the guys clips from Robert Wiene's 1919 psychological drama *The Cabinet of Dr. Caligari* and F.W. Murnau's 1922 Dracula adaptation *Nosferatu* and Fritz Lang's 1927 science-fiction master-piece *Metropolis* (with, I kid you not, a surprisingly effective score composed by Giorgio Moroder, the "Father of Disco"). It was a good session, and when we finished up at nine that evening, I was feeling pleased with myself and my students.

Halfway across the dimly illuminated yard, on my way to the Admin Building to clear security, I heard someone call my name. I turned around and looked back, and there was a figure in an orange jumpsuit in the distance, waving an arm. I figured it was one of my students with a question he hadn't thought to ask during class time, so I stood there and waited for him to catch up to me.

He caught up to me, and—you probably saw this coming—it wasn't one of my current students but John.

"For three years now," he said, "I've been hoping I'd see you again."

I looked left and right and behind me, and the yard was completely deserted, except for us. Like they say, there's never a cop around when you need one.

John was still big, still chock full o' muscles. I'm a whisker under six foot nothing myself, and I'm no ninety-eight-pound weakling, but this guy could have picked me up and snapped me in half like a stalk of celery without popping a sweat. I was pretty sure he could outrun me, too, so bolting for the exit was unlikely to save me from whatever it was I had coming.

I swallowed. "If you've got something to say to me, John," I told him, putting on a show of calmness I was *not* feeling, "here I am. Go ahead and say it."

"Oh, I have something to say to you," he said, his voice sounding like a bucket of gravel rotating inside a cement mixer.

"Did you know," he said, "I was only four months away from getting out of this hellhole when I took your class? But they tacked another three *years* onto my sentence for that robbery I talked about that day."

I hadn't known that, but it was pretty clearly a rhetorical question, so I didn't respond.

"So what I have to say to you," he said—and I took a deep breath and waited for it—"is *thank* you."

Time stopped. I was sure I couldn't possibly have heard him right.

"Excuse me?" I said.

And his mouth turned up in a brilliant smile. "Three years ago," he said, "I was an arrogant punk, and I was *not* ready to go back out into the world.

If they'd released me, I *know* I would have reoffended, and this time I'd've probably got twenty years. But I've learned a lot about myself since then, and now I'm due out in a couple of weeks, and this time I'm ready to play it straight and *stay* out. So thanks, man. You busting me was the best thing that could have happened to me at that time."

I let out the breath I hadn't realized I was holding and told him the only thing there was *to* tell him. "You're welcome," I said. "I'm not gonna say 'my pleasure,' John, because I didn't get a second's pleasure out of turning you in, but I'm glad it worked out for you."

And he stuck out his hand, and I shook it, and I think for just a moment he might actually have considered wrapping me in a bear hug, but who knows who might have been watching, so he didn't.

We went our separate ways, me to my car and home and him back to his pod—Bucky has pods, not cells—his "home" for another couple of weeks.

A few months later, I got a Christmas card from him in the mail. He enclosed a photograph of him and his new girlfriend, and inside the card, he'd written, "I'm out. I got a job. I'm clean and happy. Thanks again."

A year after that, another card and another photo, this one a wedding shot, him and the same young lady. "Still on the straight and narrow," he wrote. "Kristi says thank you, too."

And a year after *that*, the photo that came in the mail showed the two of them holding a little blanket-wrapped bundle. "Charlie's not talking yet," the message on the card read, "but you know what he'd say if he could…."

That was last Christmas. I hope John and Kristi and Charlie are still happy and healthy, and I look forward to receiving this year's card and photo.

So why am I telling *you* all this? Well, a couple of nights ago, I had dinner with my friends Mark and Ruth Bergin. Mark's an ex-cop, and now he writes crime fiction, as do I. We were swapping stories, and I told him this one.

"You have to write that up," he said. "If you don't, I will."

Well, hell, it's *my* story, not his, so I figured I'd better get it written.

Every word of it is true. Well, *almost* every word of it. All the words that *matter*, anyway.

I'm glad Mark suggested I commit it to paper. Writing it down has brought back some fond memories.

I hope you've enjoyed reading it. May all *your* jobs be perfect, and may all your Christmases be white.

Acknowledgements

Our thanks to the members of the Central Virginia chapter of Sisters in Crime, to SinC National, and to Shawn Reilly Simmons and the rest of our friends at Level Best Books. We also thank the Commonwealth of Virginia for being such a promising location for evil deeds and evil doers.

About the Contributors

KATHRYN PRATER BOMEY has published short fiction in *Black Cat Weekly* and *Shotgun Honey* and in the anthology *Three Strikes—You're Dead!* She has served as president and secretary of the Chesapeake Chapter of Sisters in Crime. As a manager of a communications team at a global nonprofit and a former journalist, her nonfiction has appeared in magazines, blogs, and daily newspapers.

www.facebook.com/KathrynPraterBomey

MARY DUTTA won the New England Crime Bake's Al Blanchard Award for her short story "The Wonderworker," which appeared in *Masthead: Best New England Crime Stories*. Her work can also be found in numerous anthologies, including the Anthony-nominated 2020 Bouchercon anthology *Land of 10,000 Thrills*. She is a member of Sisters in Crime and the Short Mystery Fiction Society and blogs at *Writers Who Kill*.

www.marydutta.com

MAY G. KENNEDY grew up in Atlanta and trained in community psychology at Georgia State University. Focusing on prevention, she has held various appointments in academic, policy, and public-health settings and was an associate professor in the Social and Behavioral Health Department at the VCU School of Medicine when she retired in 2013. "A Sum of Parts" is her first published work of fiction.

MAGGIE KING is the author of the Hazel Rose Book Group mysteries. Her short stories have appeared in the *Virginia is for Mysteries* series and in one-off anthologies, including *50 Shades of Cabernet, Deadly Southern Charm, Death*

by Cupcake, *Murder by the Glass*, and *First Comes Love, Then Comes Murder*. A member of the Short Mystery Fiction Society and a founding member of Sisters in Crime Central Virginia, she lives in Richmond.
www.maggieking.com

KRISTIN KISSKA used to be a finance geek, complete with an MBA and Wall Street pedigree, but now she is a self-proclaimed *#SuspenseGirl*. She has contributed over a dozen short stories to anthologies. Her debut novel, *The Hint of Light*, was an Agatha Award finalist for Best First Mystery Novel. A member of Mystery Writers of America, International Thriller Writers, Sisters in Crime, and James River Writers, she lives in Richmond.
www.kristinkisska.com

CINDY MARTIN chased fugitives for twenty years as a producer for *America's Most Wanted*. She travelled worldwide, wrote hundreds of TV scripts, and interviewed law enforcement and victim's families. Her short stories have appeared in the anthologies *Paradise is Deadly* and *Notorious in North Texas*. A member of Mystery Writers of America and several Sisters in Crime chapters, she's currently writing her first thriller.
www.cindymartinauthor.com

ADAM MEYER is a fiction writer and screenwriter. His short fiction has been selected for *Best American Mystery and Suspense Stories 2023*, won the Derringer Award, and been nominated for the Shamus Award. He is the editor of the upcoming anthology *In Too Deep: Crime Stories Inspired by the Songs of Genesis* and co-editor of *Hollywood Kills*, a collection of short stories by filmmakers. His screenwriting credits include more than two hundred hours of television for Lifetime, Discovery, National Geographic, and others. He's also the co-writer of *Italy: Made With Love*, an Emmy Award-winning documentary.
www.adammeyerwriter.com

K.L. MURPHY is the author of *Her Sister's Death* (a 2023 Silver Falchion finalist for Best Mystery and a Once Upon a Book Club pick), the Detective Cancini series (*A Guilty Mind, Stay of Execution,* and *The Last Sin*), *Last Girl Missing* (the first book in a new series), and several short stories. She lives in Richmond.

www.kellielarsenmurphy.com

JOSH PACHTER was the 2020 recipient of the Short Mystery Fiction Society's Golden Derringer for Lifetime Achievement. His stories appear in *EQMM, AHMM,* and elsewhere, and he is the author of the novels *Dutch Threat* and *First Week Free at the Roomy Toilet.* From his home in a Richmond suburb, he edits anthologies and translates fiction and nonfiction from multiple languages into English.

www.joshpachter.com

LEAH PRICE is the immediate past president of the Central Virginia chapter of Sisters in Crime. As **LEAH ST. JAMES**, she writes stories of good and evil, the mysteries of life, and the enduring power of love. Her published works range from romantic suspense, mystery, and police procedurals to women's fiction and even a children's fairy tale. A native of the Central Jersey Shore, she now lives in Richmond.

www.leahstjames.com

HEATHER WEIDNER has been a cop's kid, technical writer, college professor, software tester, and IT manager. She writes the Pearly Girls, Delanie Fitzgerald, Jules Keene Glamping, and Mermaid Bay Christmas Shoppe mysteries. Her short stories have appeared in various anthologies, and she has contributed non-fiction pieces to *Promophobia* and *The Secret Ingredient: A Mystery Writers' Cookbook.*

www.heatherweidner.com

CAROL WILLIS is a retired physician. She earned an MFA in fiction writing from the Vermont College of Fine Arts, and her short stories have been published in the anthology *Crimeucopia: Tales from the Back Porch* and multiple online and print magazines and journals, including *Valparaiso Fiction Review, Inlandia: A Literary Journey, Living Crue Magazine,* and *Dark Horses.* She lives in Central Virginia and writes full-time across multiple genres.

www.carolwillisauthor.com

About the Editors

JOSH PACHTER is the author of more than a hundred and twenty short crime stories, which have appeared in *EQMM, AHMM,* and many other periodicals and anthologies. His first novel, *Dutch Threat,* was published by Genius Books in 2023, and his first chapter book for younger readers, *First Week Free at the Roomy Toilet,* was published by Level Best in 2024. He also edits anthologies and translates fiction from Dutch and other languages. In 2020, he received the Short Mystery Fiction Society's Golden Derringer Award for Lifetime Achievement.

Website:
www.joshpachter.com
Social Media:
Facebook: *www.facebook.com/josh.pachter*

K.L. MURPHY is the author of *Last Girl Missing* and the forthcoming *The Murderer's Girl* (Detective Callie Forde Series), *Her Sister's Death,* a 2023 Silver Falchion finalist for Best Mystery and the January 2023 Once Upon a Book Club Pick, as well as the Detective Cancini Mystery Series including *A Guilty Mind, Stay of Execution,* and *The Last Sin.* Her short stories are featured in several anthologies. A member of Mystery Writers of America, International Thriller Writers, Sisters in Crime, and James River Writers, she makes her home in Richmond, Virginia.

Website:
kellielarsenmurphy.com
Social Media:
Instagram: @k.l._murphy
Facebook: *www.facebook.com/klmurphyauthor*

SISTERS IN CRIME-CENTRAL VIRGINIA CHAPTER
Website:
www.sistersincrimecentralvirginia.com
Social Media:
Facebook: *www.facebook.com/profile.php?id=100066526900804&ref=hl*